THE HUMAN FLY
AND OTHER STORIES

THE HUMAN FLY
AND OTHER STORIES

DISCARD

T. C. BOYLE

VIKING

ε
y
Boyle

VIKING

Published by the Penguin Group

Penguin Group (USA) Inc., 345 Hudson Street, New York, New York 10014, U.S.A.

Penguin Group (Canada), 90 Eglinton Avenue East, Suite 700, Toronto, Ontario, Canada M4P 2Y3
(a division of Pearson Penguin Canada Inc.)

Penguin Books Ltd, 80 Strand, London WC2R 0RL, England

Penguin Ireland, 25 St Stephen's Green, Dublin 2, Ireland (a division of Penguin Books Ltd)

Penguin Group (Australia), 250 Camberwell Road, Camberwell, Victoria 3124, Australia
(a division of Pearson Australia Group Pty Ltd)

Penguin Books India Pvt Ltd, 11 Community Centre, Panchsheel Park, New Delhi - 110 017, India

Penguin Group (NZ), Cnr Airborne and Rosedale Roads, Albany, Auckland 1310,
New Zealand (a division of Pearson New Zealand Ltd)

Penguin Books (South Africa) (Pty) Ltd, 24 Sturdee Avenue, Rosebank,
Johannesburg 2196, South Africa

Registered Offices: Penguin Books Ltd, 80 Strand, London WC2R 0RL, England

First published in the United States of America by Viking,
a division of Penguin Young Readers Group, 2005
Published simultaneously by Speak, an imprint of Penguin Group (USA)

1 3 5 7 9 10 8 6 4 2

Copyright © T. Coraghessan Boyle, 2005

Most of these selections appeared in *T. C. Boyle Stories* (Viking, 1999) and
After the Plague (Viking, 2001).

Page 181 is considered an extension of this copyright page.

The Library of Congress has catalogued the Speak edition as follows:

Boyle, T. Coraghessan.
The Human Fly and other stories / T.C. Boyle.
p. cm.
Contents: The Human Fly—the fog man—Rara avis—The champ—Beat—
Greasy Lake—The love of my life—Achates McNeil—56–0—The hit man—
Almost shooting an elephant—Juliana cloth—Heart of a champion.
ISBN 0-14-240363-6 (pbk.)
1. Short stories, American. [1. United States—social life and customs—20th century—Fiction.
2. Short stories.] I. Title.
PZ7.B696523Hu 2005 [Fic]—dc22 2005047436

Viking ISBN: 0-670-06054-2

Printed in the United States of America

Set in Jansen Text

For my current and former teens,
Kerrie, Milo, and Spencer

CONTENTS

THE HUMAN FLY
AND OTHER STORIES

THE HUMAN FLY

Just try to explain to anyone the art of fasting!
—Franz Kafka, "A Hunger Artist"

In the early days, before the press took him up, his outfit was pretty basic: tights and cape, plastic swim goggles and a bathing cap in the brightest shade of red he could find. The tights were red too, though they'd faded to pink in the thighs and calves and had begun to sag around the knees. He wore a pair of scuffed hightops—red, of course—and the cape, which looked as if it had last been used to line a trash can, was the color of poached salmon. He seemed to be in his thirties, though I never did find out how old he was, and he was thin, skinny, emaciated—so wasted you worried about his limbs dropping off. When he limped into the office that first afternoon, I didn't know what to think. If he brought an insect to mind, it was something spindly and frail—a daddy longlegs or one of those spidery things that scoot across the surface of the pool no matter how much chlorine the pool man dumps in.

"A gentleman here to see you," Crystal sang through the intercom.

My guard was down. I was vulnerable. I admit it. Basking in the glow of my first success (ten percent of a walk-on for Bettina Buttons, a nasally inflected twelve-year-old with pushy parents, in a picture called *Tyrannosaurus II*—no lines, but she did manage a memorable screech) and bloated with a celebratory lunch, I was feeling magnanimous, large-spirited, and saintly. Of course, the two splits of

Sangre de Cristo, 1978, might have had something to do with it. I hit the button on the intercom. "Who is it?"

"Your name, sir?" I heard Crystal ask, and then, through the crackle of static, I heard him respond in the peculiar unmodulated rumble he associated with speech.

"Pardon?" Crystal said.

"La Mosca Humana," he rumbled.

Crystal leaned into the intercom. "Uh, I think he's Mexican or something."

At that stage in my career, I had exactly three clients, all inherited from my predecessor: the aforementioned Bettina; a comic with a harelip who did harelip jokes only; and a soft-rock band called Mu, who believed they were reincarnated court musicians from the lost continent of Atlantis. The phone hadn't rung all morning and my next (and only) appointment, with Bettina's mother, grandmother, acting coach, and dietician, was at seven. "Show him in," I said grandly.

The door pushed open, and there he was. He drew himself up with as much dignity as you could expect from a grown man in a red bathing cap and pink tights, and hobbled into the office. I took in the cap, the cape, the hightops and tights, the slumped shoulders and fleshless limbs. He wore a blond mustache, droopy and unkempt, the left side of his face was badly bruised, and his nose looked as if it had been broken repeatedly—and recently. The fluorescent light glared off his goggles.

My first impulse was to call security—he looked like one of those panhandling freaks out on Hollywood Boulevard—but I resisted it. As I said, I was full of wine and feeling generous. Besides, I was so bored I'd spent the last half hour crumpling up sheets of high-fiber bond and shooting three-pointers into the wastebasket. I nodded. He nodded back. "So," I said, "what can I do for you, Mr., ah—?"

"Mosca," he rumbled, the syllables thick and muffled, as if he were trying to speak and clear his throat at the same time. "La Mosca Humana."

"The Human Fly, right?" I said, dredging up my high-school Spanish.

He looked down at the desk and then fixed his eyes on mine. "I want to be famous," he said.

How he found his way to my office, I'll never know. I've often wondered if it wasn't somebody's idea of a joke. In those days, I was nothing—I had less seniority than the guy who ran the Xerox machine—and my office was the smallest and farthest from the door of any in the agency. I was expected to get by with two phone lines, one secretary, and a workspace not much bigger than a couple of good-sized refrigerator boxes. There were no Utrillos or Demuths on my walls. I didn't even have a window.

I understood that the man hovering over my desk was a nutcase, but there was more to it than that. I could see that he had something—a dignity, a sad elemental presence—that gave the lie to his silly outfit. I felt uneasy under his gaze. "Don't we all," I said.

"No, no," he insisted, "you don't understand," and he pulled a battered manila envelope from the folds of his cape. "Here," he said, "look."

The envelope contained his press clippings, a good handful of them, yellowed and crumbling, bleached of print. All but one were in Spanish. I adjusted the desk lamp, squinted hard. The datelines were from places like Chetumal, Tuxtla, Hidalgo, Tehuantepec. As best I could make out, he'd been part of a Mexican circus. The sole clipping in English was from the "Metro" section of the *Los Angeles Times:* MAN ARRESTED FOR SCALING ARCO TOWER.

I read the first line—"A man known only as 'The Human Fly' "—and I was hooked. What a concept: *a man known only as the Human Fly!* It was priceless. Reading on, I began to see him in a new light: the costume, the limp, the bruises. This was a man who'd climbed twenty stories with nothing more than a couple pieces of rope and his fingernails. A man who defied the authorities, defied death—my mind was doing backflips; we could run with this one, oh, yes, indeed. Forget your Rambos and Conans, this guy was the real thing.

"Five billion of us monkey on the planet," he said in his choked, moribund tones, "I want to make my mark."

I looked up in awe. I saw him on Carson, Letterman, grappling his way to the top of the Bonaventure Hotel, hurtling Niagara in a barrel, starring in his own series. I tried to calm myself. "Uh, your face," I said, and I made a broad gesture that took in the peach-colored bruise, the ravaged nose and stiffened leg, "what happened?"

For the first time, he smiled. His teeth were stained and ragged; his eyes flared behind the cracked plastic lenses of the goggles. "An accident," he said.

As it turned out, he wasn't Mexican at all—he was Hungarian. I saw my mistake when he peeled back the goggles and bathing cap. A fine band of skin as blanched and waxen as the cap of a mushroom outlined his ears, his hairline, the back of his neck, dead-white against the sun-burnished oval of his face. His eyes were a pale watery blue and the hair beneath the cap was as wispy and colorless as the strands of his mustache. His name was Zoltan Mindszenty, and he'd come to Los Angeles to live with his uncle when the Russian tanks rolled through Budapest in 1956. He'd learned English, Spanish and baseball, practiced fire-eating and tightrope-walking in his spare time, graduated at the top of his high-school class, and operated a forklift in a cannery that produced refried beans and cactus salad. At the age of nineteen he joined the Quesadilla Brothers' Circus and saw the world. Or at least that part of it bounded by California, Arizona, New Mexico, and Texas to the north and Belize and Guatemala to the south. Now he wanted to be famous.

He moved fast. Two days after I'd agreed to represent him he made the eyewitness news on all three major networks when he suspended himself in a mesh bag from the twenty-second floor of the Sumitomo Building and refused to come down.

Terrific. The only problem was that he didn't bother to tell me about it. I was choking down a quick salad lunch—avocado and sprouts on a garlic-cheese croissant—already running late for an audition I'd set up for my harelipped comedian—when the phone rang. It was a Lieutenant Peachtree of the LAPD. "Listen," the lieutenant hissed, "if this is a publicity stunt . . ." and he trailed off, leaving the threat—heavy ire, the violation of penal codes, the arcane and merciless measures taken to deal with accessories—unspoken.

"Pardon?"

"The nutball up on the Sumitomo Building. Your client."

Comprehension washed over me. My first thought was to deny the connection, but instead I found myself stammering, "But, but how did you get my name?"

Terse and efficient, a living police report, Peachtree gave me the details. One of his men, hanging out of a window on the twenty-first floor, had pleaded with Zoltan to come down. "I am the Human Fly," Zoltan rumbled in response as the wind snapped and the traffic sizzled below, "you want to talk to me, call my agent."

"Twenty minutes," Peachtree added, and his tone was as flat and unforgiving as the drop of a guillotine, "I want you down here. Five minutes after that I want this clown in the back of the nearest patrol car—is that understood?"

It was. Perfectly. And twenty minutes later, with the help of an Officer Dientes, a screaming siren, and several hundred alert motorists who fell away from us on the freeway like swatted flies, I was taking the breeze on the twenty-first floor of the Sumitomo Building. Two of Peachtree's men gripped my legs and eased my torso out onto the slick glassy plane of the building's façade.

I was sick with fear. Before me lay the immensity of the city, its jaws and molars exposed. Above was the murky sky, half a dozen pigeons on a ledge, and Zoltan, bundled up like a sack of grapefruit and calmly perusing a paperback thriller. I choked back the remains of the croissant and cleared my throat. "Zoltan!" I shouted, the wind snatching the words from my lips and flinging them away. "Zoltan, what are you doing up there?"

There was a movement from the bag above me, Zoltan stirring himself like a great leathery fruit bat unfolding its wings, and then his skinny legs and outsized feet emerged from their confinement as the bag swayed gently in the breeze. He peered down at me, the goggles aflame with the sun, and gave me a sour look. "You're supposed to be my agent, and you have to ask me that?"

"It's a stunt, then—is that it?" I shouted.

He turned his face away, and the glare of the goggles died. He wouldn't answer me. Behind me, I could hear Peachtree's crisp, efficient tones: "Tell him he's going to jail."

"They're going to lock you up. They're not kidding."

For a long moment, he didn't respond. Then the goggles caught the sun again and he turned to me. "I want the TV people, Tricia Toyota, *Action News*, the works."

I began to feel dizzy. The pavement below, with its toy cars and its clots of tiny people, seemed to rush up at me and recede again in a pulsing wave. I felt Peachtree's men relax their grip. "They won't come!" I gasped, clutching the windowframe so desperately my fingers went numb. "They can't. It's network policy." It was true, as far as I knew. Every flake in the country would be out on that ledge if they thought they could get a ten-second clip on the evening news.

Zoltan was unimpressed. "TV," he rumbled into the wind, "or I stay here till you see the white of my bone."

I believed him.

As it turned out, he stayed there, aloft, for two weeks. And for some reason—because he was intractable, absurd, mad beyond hope or redemption—the press couldn't get enough of it. TV included. How he passed the time, what he ate, how he relieved himself, no one knew. He was just a presence, a distant speck in a mesh sack, the faintest intrusion of reality on the clear smooth towering face of the Sumitomo Building. Peachtree tried to get him down, of course—

harassing him with helicopters, sending a squad of window cleaners, firemen, and lederhosen up after him—but nothing worked. If anyone got close to him, Zoltan would emerge from his cocoon, cling to the seamless face of the building, and float—float like a big red fly—to a new position.

Finally, after the two weeks were up—two weeks during which my phone never stopped ringing, by the way—he decided to come down. Did he climb in the nearest window and take the elevator? No, not Zoltan. He backed down, inch by inch, uncannily turning up finger- and toeholds where none existed. He sprang the last fifteen feet to the ground, tumbled like a skydiver, and came up in the grip of a dozen policemen. There was a barricade up, streets were blocked, hundreds of spectators had gathered. As they were hustling him to a patrol car, the media people converged on him. Was it a protest? they wanted to know. A hunger strike? What did it mean?

He turned to them, the goggles steamed over, pigeon feathers and flecks of airborne debris clinging to his cape. His legs were like sticks, his face nearly black with sun and soot. "I want to be famous," he said.

"A DC-10?"

Zoltan nodded. "The bigger, the better," he rumbled.

It was the day after he'd decamped from the face of the Sumitomo Building and we were in my office, discussing the next project. (I'd bailed him out myself, though the figure was right up there with what you'd expect for a serial killer. There were fourteen charges against him, ranging from trespassing to creating a public nuisance and refusing the reasonable request of a police officer to indecent exposure. I had to call in every favor that was ever owed to me and go down on my knees to Sol Bankoff, the head of the agency, to raise the cash.) Zoltan was wearing the outfit I'd had specially made for him: new tights, a black silk cape without a wrinkle in it, a pair of Air Jordan basketball shoes in red and black, and most important of all, a red leather aviator's cap and goggles. Now he looked less like a geriatric at a health spa and more like the sort of fearless daredevil/superhero the public could relate to.

"But Zoltan," I pleaded, "those things go five hundred miles an hour. You'd be ripped to pieces. Climbing buildings is one thing, but this is insane. It's suicidal."

He was slouched in the chair, one skinny leg thrown over the other. "The Human Fly can survive anything," he droned in his lifeless voice. He was staring at the floor, and now he lifted his head. "Besides, you think the public have any respect for me if I don't lay it all on line?"

He had a point. But strapping yourself to the wing of a DC-10 made about as much sense as taking lunch at a sidewalk café in Beirut. "Okay," I said, "you're right. But you've got to draw the line somewhere. What good's it going to do you to be famous if you're dead?"

Zoltan shrugged.

"I mean already, just with the Sumitomo thing, I can book you on half the talk shows in the country. . . ."

He rose shakily to his feet, lifted his hand, and let it drop. Two weeks on the face of the Sumitomo Building with no apparent source of nourishment hadn't done him any good. If he was skinny before, he was nothing now—a shadow, a ghost, a pair of tights stuffed with straw. "Set it up," he rumbled, the words riding up out of the depths of his sunken abdomen, "I talk when I got something to talk about."

It took me a week. I called every airline in the directory, listened to a lifetime's worth of holding jingles, and talked to everyone from the forklift operator at KLM to the president and CEO of Texas Air. I was met by scorn, hostility, disbelief, and naked contempt. Finally I got hold of the schedules manager of Aero Masoquisto, the Ecuadorian national airline. It was going to cost me, he said, but he could hold up the regular weekly flight to Quito for a few hours while Zoltan strapped himself to the wing and took a couple passes round the airport. He suggested an airstrip outside Tijuana, where the officials would look the other way. For a price, of course.

Of course.

I went to Sol again. I was prepared to press my forehead to the floor, shine his shoes, anything—but he surprised me. "I'll front the money," he rasped, his voice ruined from forty years of whispering into the telephone, "no problem." Sol was seventy, looked fifty, and he'd had his own table in the Polo Lounge since before I was born. "If he bags it," he said, his voice as dry as a husk, "we got the rights to his life story and we'll do a paperback/miniseries/action-figure tie-in. Just get him to sign this, that's all." He slid a contract across the table. "And if he makes it, which I doubt—I mean I've seen some crazies in my time, but this guy is something else—if he makes it, we'll have a million and a half offers for him. Either way, we make out, right?"

"Right," I said, but I was thinking of Zoltan, his brittle limbs pressed to the unyielding metal, the terrible pull of the G-forces, and the cyclonic blast of the wind. What chance did he have?

Sol cleared his throat, shook a few lozenges into his fist, and rattled them like dice. "Your job," he said, "is to make sure the press shows up. No sense in this nimrod bagging it for nothing, right?"

I felt something clench in my gut.

Sol repeated himself, "Right?"

"Right," I said.

Zoltan was in full regalia as we boarded the plane at LAX, along with a handful of reporters and photographers and a hundred grim-looking Ecuadorians with plastic bags full of disposable diapers, cosmetics, and penlight batteries. The plan was for the pilot to announce a minor problem—a clogged air-conditioning vent or a broken handle in the flush toilet; we didn't want to panic anybody—and an unscheduled stop to repair it. Once on the ground, the passengers would be asked to disembark and we'd offer them free drinks in the spacious terminal while the plane taxied out of sight and Zoltan did his thing.

Problem was, there was no terminal. The landing strip looked as if it had been bombed during the Mexican Revolution, it was a hundred degrees inside the airplane and one hundred and twenty out on the asphalt, and all I could see was heat haze and prickly-pear cactus. "What do you want to do?" I asked Zoltan.

Zoltan turned to me, already fumbling with his chin strap. "It's perfect," he whispered, and then he was out in the aisle, waving his arms and whistling for the passengers' attention. When they quieted down, he spoke to them in Spanish, the words coming so fast you might have thought he was a Mexican disc jockey, his voice riding on a current of emotion he never approached in English. I don't know what he said—he could have been exhorting them to hijack the plane, for all I knew—but the effect was dramatic. When he finished, they rose to their feet and cheered.

With a flourish, Zoltan threw open the emergency exit over the wing and began his preparations. Flashbulbs popped, reporters hung out the door and shouted questions at him—Had this ever been attempted before? Did he have his will made out? How high was he planning to go?—and the passengers pressed their faces to the windows. I'd brought along a TV crew to capture the death-defying feat for syndication, and they set up one camera on the ground while the other shot through the window.

Zoltan didn't waste any time. He buckled what looked like a huge leather truss around the girth of the wing, strapped himself into the pouch attached to it, tightened his chin strap a final time, and then gave me the thumbs-up sign. My heart was hammering. A dry wind breathed through the open window. The heat was like a fist in my face. "You're sure you want to go through with this?" I yelled.

"One hundred percent, A-OK," Zoltan shouted, grinning as the reporters crowded round me in the narrow passageway. Then the pilot said something in Spanish and the flight attendants pulled the window shut, fastened the bolts, and told us to take our seats. A moment later the big engines roared to life and we were hurtling down the runway. I could barely stand to look. At best, I consider flying an unavoidable necessity, a time to resurrect forgotten prayers and contemplate the end of all joy in a twisted howling heap of machinery; at worst, I rank it right up there with psychotic episodes and torture at the hands of malevolent strangers. I felt the wheels lift off, heard a shout from the passengers, and there he was—Zoltan—clinging to the trembling thunderous wing like a second coat of paint.

It was a heady moment, transcendent, the camera whirring, the passengers cheering, Zoltan's greatness a part of us all. This was an event, a once-in-a-lifetime thing, like watching Hank Aaron stroke his seven hundred fifteenth homer or Neil Armstrong step out onto the surface of the moon. We forgot the heat, forgot the roar of the engines, forgot ourselves. He's doing it, I thought, he's actually doing it. And I truly think he would have pulled it off, if—well, it was one of those things no one could have foreseen. Bad luck, that's all.

What happened was this: just as the pilot was coming in for his final approach, a big black bird—a buzzard, somebody said—loomed up out of nowhere and slammed into Zoltan with a thump that reverberated throughout the plane. The whole thing took maybe half a second. This black bundle appears, there's a thump, and next thing Zoltan's goggles are gone and he's covered from head to toe in raw meat and feathers.

A gasp went through the cabin. Babies began to mewl, grown men burst into tears, a nun fainted. My eyes were riveted on Zoltan. He lay limp in his truss while the hot air sliced over the wing, and the jagged yellow mountains, the prickly pear, and the pocked landing strip rushed past him like the backdrop of an old movie. The plane was still rolling when we threw open the emergency exit and staggered out onto the wing. The copilot was ahead of me, a reporter on my heels. "Zoltan!" I cried, scared and sick and trembling. "Zoltan, are you all right?"

There was no answer. Zoltan's head lolled against the flat hard surface of the wing and his eyes were closed, sunk deep behind the wrinkled flaps of his lids. There was blood everywhere. I bent to tear at the straps of the aviator's cap, my mind racing, thinking alternately of mouth-to-mouth and the medical team I should have thought to bring along, when an urgent voice spoke at my back. "Perdóneme, perdóneme, I yam a doaktor."

One of the passengers, a wizened little man in Mickey Mouse T-shirt and Bermudas, knelt over Zoltan, shoving back his eyelids and feeling for his pulse. There were shouts behind me. The wing was as hot as the surface of a frying pan. "Jes, I yam getting a pulse," the doctor announced and then Zoltan winked open an eye. "Hey," he rumbled, "am I famous yet?"

Zoltan was right: the airplane stunt fired the imagination of the country. The wire services picked it up, the news magazines ran stories—there was even a bit on the CBS evening news. A week later the *National Enquirer* was calling him the reincarnation of Houdini and the *Star* was speculating about his love life. I booked him on the talk-show circuit, and while he might not have had much to say, he just about oozed charisma. He appeared on the Carson show in his trademark outfit, goggles and all, limping and with his arm in a sling (he'd suffered a minor concussion, a shoulder separation, and a fractured kneecap when the bird hit him). Johnny asked him what it was like out there on the wing and Zoltan said: "Loud." And what was it like spending two weeks on the face of the Sumitomo Building? "Boring," Zoltan rumbled. But Carson segued into a couple of airline jokes ("Have you heard the new slogan for China Airlines?" Pause. "You've seen us drive, now watch us fly") and the audience ate it up. Offers poured in from promoters, producers, book editors, and toy manufacturers. I was able to book David Mugillo, my harelipped comedian, on Zoltan's coattails, and when we did the Carson show we got Bettina Buttons on for three minutes of nasal simpering about

Tyrannosaurus II and how educational an experience it was for her to work with such a sensitive and caring director as so-and-so.

Zoltan had arrived.

A week after his triumph on *The Tonight Show* he hobbled into the office, the cape stained and torn, tights gone in the knees. He brought a distinctive smell with him—the smell of pissed-over gutters and fermenting Dumpsters—and for the first time I began to understand why he'd never given me an address or a phone number. ("You want me," he said, "leave a message with Ramón at Jiffy Cleaners.") All at once I had a vision of him slinging his grapefruit sack from the nearest drainpipe and curling up for the night. "Zoltan," I said, "are you okay? You need some cash? A place to stay?"

He sat heavily in the chair across from me. Behind him, on the wall, was an oil painting of an open window, a gift from Mu's bass player. Zoltan waved me off. Then, with a weary gesture, he reached up and removed the cap and goggles. I was shocked. His hair was practically gone and his face was as seamed and scarred as an old hockey puck. He looked about a hundred and twelve. He said nothing.

"Well," I said, to break the silence, "you got your wish. You made it." I lifted a stack of correspondence from the desk and waved it at him. "You're famous."

Zoltan turned his head and spat on the floor. "Famous," he mocked. "Fidel Castro is famous. Irving Berlin. Evel Knievel." His rumble had turned bitter. "Peterbilt," he said suddenly.

This last took me by surprise. I'd been thinking of consolatory platitudes, and all I could do was echo him weakly: "Peterbilt?"

"I want the biggest rig going. The loudest, the dirtiest."

I wasn't following him.

"Maine to L.A.," he rumbled.

"You're going to drive it?"

He stood shakily, fought his way back into the cap, and lowered the goggles. "Shit," he spat, "I ride the axle."

■ ■ ■

I tried to talk him out of it. "Think of the fumes," I said, "the road hazards. Potholes, dead dogs, mufflers. You'll be two feet off the pavement, going seventy-five, eighty miles an hour. Christ, a cardboard box'll tear you apart."

He wouldn't listen. Not only was he going through with it, but he wanted to coordinate it so that he ended up in Pasadena, for the swap meet at the Rose Bowl. There he would emerge from beneath the truck, wheel a motorcycle out of the back, roar up a ramp, and sail over twenty-six big rigs lined up fender to fender in the middle of the parking lot.

I asked Sol about it. Advance contracts had already made back the money he'd laid out for the airplane thing ten times over. And now we could line up backers. "Get him to wear a Pirelli patch on his cape," Sol rasped, "it's money in the bank."

Easy for Sol to say, but I was having problems with the whole business. This wasn't a plastic dinosaur on a movie lot or a stinko audience at the Improv, this was flesh and blood we were talking about here, a human life. Zoltan wasn't healthy—in mind or body. The risks he took weren't healthy. His ambition wasn't healthy. And if I went along with him, I was no better than Sol, a mercenary, a huckster who'd watch a man die for ten percent of the action. For a day or two I stayed away from the office, brooding around the kitchen in my slippers. In the end, though, I talked myself into it— Zoltan was going to do it with or without me. And who knew what kind of bloodsucker he'd wind up with next?

I hired a PR firm, got a major trucking company to carry him for the goodwill and free publicity, and told myself it was for the best. I'd ride in the cab with the driver, keep him awake, watch over Zoltan personally. And of course I didn't know how it was going to turn out—Zoltan *was* amazing, and if anyone could pull it off, he could—and I thought of the Sumitomo Building and Aero Masoquisto and hoped for the best.

■ ■ ■

We left Bangor in a cold drizzle on a morning that could have served as the backdrop for a low-budget horror picture: full-bellied clouds, gloom, mist, nose running cold. By the time we reached Portland the drizzle had begun to crust on the windshield wipers; before we reached New Hampshire it was sleet. The driver was an American Indian by the name of Mink—no middle name, no surname, just Mink. He weighed close to five hundred pounds and he wore his hair in a single braided coil that hung to his belt loops in back. The other driver, whose name was Steve, was asleep in the compartment behind the cab. "Listen, Mink," I said, the windshield wipers beating methodically at the crust, tires hissing beneath us, "maybe you should pull over so we can check on Zoltan."

Mink shifted his enormous bulk in the seat. "What, the Fly?" he said. "No sweat. That guy is like amazing. I seen that thing with the airplane. He can survive that, he's got no problem with this rig—long's I don't hit nothin'."

The words were barely out of his mouth when an animal—a huge brown thing like a cow on stilts—materialized out of the mist. Startled, Mink jerked the wheel, the truck went into a skid, there was a jolt like an earthquake, and the cow on stilts was gone, sucked under the front bumper like a scrap of food sucked down a drain. When we finally came to a stop a hundred yards up the road, the trailer was perpendicular to the cab and Mink's hands were locked to the wheel.

"What happened?" I said.

"Moose," Mink breathed, adding a soft breathless curse. "We hit a fuckin' moose."

In the next instant I was down and out of the cab, racing the length of the trailer, and shouting Zoltan's name. Earlier, in the cold dawn of Bangor, I'd watched him stretch out his mesh bag and suspend it like a trampoline from the trailer's undercarriage, just ahead of the rear wheels. He'd waved to the reporters gathered in the drizzle, ducked beneath the trailer, and climbed into the bag.

Now, my heart banging, I wondered what a moose might have done to so tenuous an arrangement. "Zoltan!" I shouted, going down on my knees to peer into the gloom beneath the trailer.

There was no moose. Zoltan's cocoon was still intact, and so was he. He was lying there on his side, a thin fetal lump rounding out of the steel and grime. "What?" he rumbled.

I asked him the question I always seemed to be asking him: was he all right?

It took him a moment—he was working his hand free—and then he gave me the thumbs-up sign. "A-OK," he said.

The rest of the trip—through the icy Midwest, the wind-torn Rockies, and the scorching strip between Tucson and Gila Bend—was uneventful. For me, anyway. I alternately slept, ate truckstop fare designed to remove the lining of your stomach, and listened to Mink or Steve—their conversation was interchangeable—rhapsodize about Harleys, IROC Camaros, and women who went down on all fours and had "Truckers' Delite" tattooed across their buttocks. For Zoltan, it was business as usual. If he suffered from the cold, the heat, the tumbleweeds, beer cans, and fast-food containers that ricocheted off his poor lean scrag of a body day and night, he never mentioned it. True to form, he refused food and drink, though I suspected he must have had something concealed in his cape, and he never climbed down out of his cocoon, not even to move his bowels. Three days and three nights after we'd left Maine, we wheeled the big rig through the streets of Pasadena and into the parking lot outside the Rose Bowl, right on schedule.

There was a fair-sized crowd gathered, though there was no telling whether they'd come for the swap meet, the heavy-metal band we'd hired to give some punch to Zoltan's performance, or the stunt itself, but then who cared? They were there. As were the *Action News* team, the souvenir hawkers and hot-dog vendors. Grunting, his face beaded with sweat, Mink guided the truck into place alongside the twenty-five others, straining to get it as close as possible: an inch could mean the difference between life and death for Zoltan, and we all knew it.

I led a knot of cameramen to the rear of the truck so they could get some tape of Zoltan crawling out of his grapefruit bag. When they were all gathered, he stirred himself, shaking off the froth of insects and road grime, the scraps of paper and cellophane, placing first one bony foot and then the other on the pavement. His eyes were feverish behind the lenses of the goggles and when he lurched out from under the truck I had to catch his arm to prevent him from falling. "So how does it feel to conquer the roadways?" asked a microphone-jabbing reporter with moussed hair and flawless teeth. "What was the worst moment?" asked another.

Zoltan's legs were rubber. He reeked of diesel fuel, his cape was in tatters, his face smeared with sweat and grease. "Twenty-six truck," he rumbled. "The Human Fly is invincible."

And then the band started in—smokebombs, megadecibels, sub-human screeches, the works—and I led Zoltan to his dressing room. He refused a shower, but allowed the makeup girl to sponge off his face and hands. We had to cut the old outfit off him—he was too exhausted to undress himself—and then the girl helped him into the brand-new one I'd provided for the occasion. "Twenty-six truck," he kept mumbling to himself, "A-OK."

I wanted him to call it off. I did. He wasn't in his right mind, anybody could see that. And he was exhausted, beat, as starved and helpless as a refugee. He wouldn't hear of it. "Twenty-six truck," he rumbled, and when I put through a frantic last-minute call to Sol, Sol nearly swallowed the phone. "Damn straight he's going for it!" he shouted. "We got sponsors lined up here. ABC Sports wants to see the tape, for christsake." There was an outraged silence punctuated by the click of throat lozenges, and then Sol cut the connection.

Ultimately, Zoltan went for it. Mink threw open the trailer door, Zoltan fired up the motorcycle—a specially modified Harley Sportster with gas shocks and a bored engine—and one of our people signaled the band to cut it short. The effect was dynamic, the band cutting back suddenly to a punchy drum-and-bass thing and the growl of the big bike coming on in counterpoint . . . and then Zoltan sprang from the back of the trailer, his cape stiff with the breeze, goggles flashing, tires squealing. He made three circuits of the lot, coming in close on the line of trucks, dodging away from the ramp, hunched low and flapping over the handlebars. Every eye was on him. Suddenly he raised a bony fist in the air, swerved wide of the trucks in a great arcing loop that took him to the far end of the lot, and made a run for the ramp.

He was a blur, he was nothing, he was invisible, a rush of motion above the scream of the engine. I saw something—a shadow—launch itself into the thick brown air, cab after cab receding beneath it, the glint of chrome in the sun, fifteen trucks, twenty, twenty-five, and then the sight that haunts me to this day. Suddenly the shadow was gone and a blemish appeared on the broad side panel of the last truck, the one we'd taken across country, Mink's truck, and then, simultaneous with it, there was the noise. A single booming reverberation, as if the world's biggest drum had exploded, followed by the abrupt cessation of the motorcycle's roar and the sad tumbling clatter of dissociated metal.

We had medical help this time, of course, the best available: paramedics, trauma teams, ambulances. None of it did any good. When I pushed through the circle of people around him, Zoltan was lying there on the pavement like a bundle of broken twigs. The cape was twisted round his neck, and his limbs—the sorry fleshless sticks of his arms and legs—were skewed like a doll's. I bent over him as the paramedics brought up the stretcher. "Twenty-five truck next time," he whispered, "promise me." There was blood in his ears, his nostrils, his eye sockets. "Yes," I said, "yes. Twenty-five."

"No worries," he choked as they slid the stretcher under him, "the Human Fly . . . can survive . . . anything."

We buried him three days later.

It was a lonely affair, as funerals go. The uncle, a man in his seventies with the sad scrawl of time on his face, was the only mourner. The press stayed away, though the videotape of Zoltan's finale was shown repeatedly over the air and the freeze-frame photos appeared in half the newspapers in the country. I was shaken by the whole thing. Sol gave me a week off and I did some soul-searching. For a while I thought of giving up the entertainment business altogether, but I was pulled back into it despite myself. Everybody, it seemed, wanted a piece of Zoltan. And as I sat down to sort through the letters, telegrams, and urgent callback messages, the phone ringing unceasingly, the sun flooding the windows of my new well-appointed and high-flown office, I began to realize that I owed it to Zoltan to pursue them. This was what he'd wanted, after all.

We settled finally on the animated series, with the usual tie-ins. I knew the producer—Sol couldn't say enough about him—and I knew he'd do quality work. Sure enough, the show premiered number one in its timeslot and it's been there ever since. Sometimes I'll get up early on a Saturday morning just to tune in, to watch the jerky figures move against a backdrop of greed and corruption, the Human Fly ascendant, incorruptible, climbing hand over hand to the top.

(1988)

THE FOG MAN

He came twice a week, rattling through the development in an army-surplus jeep, laying down a roiling smoke screen that melted the trees into oblivion, flattened hills and swallowed up houses, erased Fords, Chevies, and Studebakers as if they were as insubstantial as the air itself, and otherwise transformed the world to our satisfaction. Shrubs became dinosaurs, lampposts giraffes, the blacktop of the streets seethed like the surface of the swamp primeval. Our fathers stood there on their emerald lawns, hoses dripping, and they waved languidly or turned their backs to shoot a sparkling burst at the flower beds or forsythias. We took to our bikes, supercharged with the excitement of it, and we ran just behind him, the fog man, wheeling in and out of the tight billowing clouds like fighter pilots slashing across the sky or Grand Prix racers nosing in for the lead on that final excruciating lap. He gave us nothing except those moments of transfiguration, but we chased him as single-mindedly as we chased the ice-cream man in his tinkling white truck full of Drumsticks and Eskimo Pies, chased him till he'd completed his tour of the six connecting streets of the development—up one side and down the other—and lurched across the highway, trailing smoke, for the next.

And then the smoke settled, clinging to the dewy wet grass, the

odor of smoldering briquettes fought over the top of the sweet nar-
cotic smell of it, and we were gone, disseminated, slammed behind
identical screen doors, in our identical houses, for the comfort and
magic of the TV. My father was there, always there, propped up in
his recliner, one hand over his eyes to mask an imaginary glare, the
other clutched round his sweating drink. My mother was there too,
legs tucked under her on the couch, the newspaper spread in her lap,
her drink on the cluttered table beside her.

"The fog man was just here," I would announce. I didn't expect
a response, really—it was just something to say. The show on TV
was about a smiling family. All the shows were about smiling families. My mother would nod.

One night I appended a question. "He's spraying for bugs,
right?" This much I knew, this much had been explained to me, but
I wanted confirmation, affirmation, I wanted reason and meaning to
illuminate my life.

My father said nothing. My mother looked up. "Mosquitoes."

"Yeah, that's what I thought—but how come there's so many of
them then? They bit right through my shirt on the front porch."

My mother tapped at her cigarette, took a sip of her drink. "You
can't get them all," she said.

It was at about this time that the local power company opened the
world's first atomic power plant at Indian Point. Ten years earlier
nuclear fission had been an instrument of war and destruction; now
it was safe, manageable; now it would warm our houses and light our
lights and power our hi-fis and toasters and dishwashers. The electric company took pains to ensure that the community saw it that
way. It was called public relations.

I didn't know the term then. I was eleven years old, in my first
week of my last year of elementary school, and on my way to the
power plant in a school bus crammed to the yawning windows with
my excitable classmates. This was known as a field trip. The previ-

ous year we'd been to a farm in Brewster and the Museum of Natural History in New York. We were starting early this year, but it was all due to the fact of this astonishing new technological force set down amongst us, this revolution in the production of electricity and the streamlining of our lives. We didn't know what to expect.

The bus rumbled and belched fumes. I sat on the hard cracked leatherette seat beside Casper Mendelson and watched the great gray concrete dome rise up out of the clutch of the trees, dominating the point and the placid broad fish-stinking river beyond it. It was impressive, this huge structure inside of which the titanic forces of the universe were pared down to size. Casper said that it could blow up, like the bomb they'd dropped on the Japanese, and that it would take all of Peterskill and Westchester with it. The river would turn to steam and there'd be nothing left but a crater the size of the Grand Canyon and we'd all be melted in our beds. I gaped out the window at the thing, awestruck, the big dome keeping a lid on all that seething complexity, and I was impressed, but I couldn't help thinking of the point's previous incarnation as an amusement park, a place of strung lights, cotton candy, and carousels. Now there was this gray dome.

They led us into a little brightly lit building full of colorful exhibits, where we handled things that were meant to be handled, scuffed the gleaming linoleum floors, and watched an animated short in which Johnny Atom splits himself in two and saves the world by creating electricity. The whole thing was pretty dull, aside from the dome itself and what Casper had said about it, and within the hour my classmates were filling the place with the roar of a stampede, breaking the handles off things, sobbing, skipping, playing tag, and wondering seriously about lunch—which, as it turned out, we were to have back at school, in the cafeteria, after which we were expected to return to our classrooms and discuss what we'd learned on our field trip.

I remember the day for the impression that imposing gray dome made on me, but also because it was the first chance I got to have a look at Maki Duryea, the new girl who'd been assigned to the other sixth-grade section. Maki was black—or not simply black, but black and Oriental both. Her father had been stationed in Osaka during the occupation; her mother was Japanese. I watched her surreptitiously that morning as I sat in the rear of the bus with Casper. She was somewhere in the middle, sitting beside Donna Siprelle, a girl I'd known all my life. All I could make out was the back of her head, but that was enough, that alone was a revelation. Her hair was an absolute, unalloyed, interstellar black, and it disappeared behind the jutting high ridge of the seat back as if it might go on forever. It had hung iron straight when we first climbed aboard the bus that morning, but on the way back it was transformed, a leaping electric snarl that engulfed the seat and eclipsed the neat little ball of yellow curls that clung to the back of Donna Siprelle's head. "Maki Duryea, Maki Duryea," Casper began to chant, though no one could hear him but me in the pandemonium of that preprandial school bus. Annoyed, I poked him with a savage elbow but he kept it up, louder now, to spite me.

There were no blacks in our school, there were no Asians or Hispanics. Italians, Poles, Jews, Irish, the descendants of the valley's Dutch and English settlers, these we had, these we were, but Maki Duryea was the first black—and the first Asian. Casper's father was Jewish, his mother a Polish Catholic. Casper had the soaring IQ of a genius, but he was odd, skewed in some deep essential way that set him apart from the rest of us. He was the first to masturbate, the first to drink and smoke, though he cared for neither. He caused a panic throughout the school when he turned up missing one day after lunch and was found, after a room-by-room, locker-by-locker search, calmly reading on the fire escape; he burst from his chair at the back of the classroom once and did fifty frantic squat-thrusts in front of the hapless teacher and then blew on his thumb till he passed out. He was my best friend.

He turned to me then, on the bus, and broke off his chant. His eyes were the color of the big concrete dome, his head was shaved to a transparent stubble. "She stinks," he said, grinning wildly, his eyes leaping at my own. "Maki Duryea, Maki Duryea, Maki Duryea"—he took up the chant again before subsiding into giggles. "They don't smell like we do."

My family was Irish. Irish, that's all I knew. A shirt was cotton or it was wool. We were Irish. No one talked about it, there was no exotic language spoken in the house, no ethnic dress or cuisine, we didn't go to church. There was only my grandfather.

He came that year for Thanksgiving, a short big-bellied man with close-cropped white hair and glancing white eyebrows and a trace of something in his speech I hadn't heard before—or if I had it was in some old out-of-focus movie dredged up for the TV screen, nothing I would have remembered. My grandmother came too. She was spindly, emaciated, her skin blistered with shingles, a diabetic who couldn't have weighed more than ninety pounds, but there was joy in her and it was infectious. My father, her son, woke up. A festive air took hold of the house.

My grandfather, who years later dressed in a suit for my father's funeral and was mistaken for a banker, had had a heart attack and he wasn't drinking. Or rather, he was strictly enjoined from drinking, and my parents, who drank themselves, drank a lot, drank too much, took pains to secrete the liquor supply. Every bottle was removed from the cabinet, even the odd things that hadn't been touched in years—except by me, when I furtively unscrewed the cap of this or that and took a sniff or touched my tongue tentatively to the cold hard glass aperture—and the beer disappeared from the refrigerator. I didn't know what the big deal was. Liquor was there, a fact of life, it was unpleasant and adults indulged in it as they indulged in any number of bizarre and unsatisfactory practices. I kicked a football around the rock-hard frozen lawn.

And then one afternoon—it was a day or two before Thanksgiving and my grandparents had been with us a week—I came in off the front lawn, my fingers numb and nose running, and the house was in an uproar. A chair was overturned in the corner, the coffee table was slowly listing over a crippled leg, and my grandmother was on the floor, frail, bunched, a bundle of sticks dropped there in a windstorm. My grandfather stood over her, red-faced and raging, while my mother snatched at his elbow like a woman tumbling over the edge of a cliff. My father wasn't home from work yet. I stood there in the doorway, numb from the embrace of the wind, and heard the inarticulate cries of those two women against the oddly inflected roars of that man, and I backed out the door and pulled it closed behind me.

The next day my grandfather, sixty-eight years old and stiff in the knees, walked two miles in twenty-degree weather to Peterskill, to the nearest liquor store. It was dark, suppertime, and we didn't know where he was. "He just went out for a walk," my mother said. Then the phone rang. It was the neighbor two doors down. There was a man passed out in her front yard—somebody said we knew him. Did we?

I spent the next two days—Thanksgiving and the day after—camping in the sorry patch of woods at the end of the development. I wasn't running away, nothing as decisive or extreme as that—I was just camping, that was all. I gnawed cold turkey up there in the woods, lifted congealed stuffing to my mouth with deadened fingers. In the night I lay shivering in my blankets, never colder before or since.

We were Irish. I was Irish.

That winter, like all winters in those days, was interminable, locked up in the grip of frozen slush and exhaust-blackened snow. The dead dark hours of school were penance for some crime we hadn't yet committed. The TV went on at three-thirty when we got home from

school, and it was still on when we went to bed at nine. I played basketball that winter in a league organized by some of the fathers in
the development, and three times a week I walked home from the
fungus-infested gym with a crust of frozen sweat in my hair. I grew
an inch and a half, I let my crewcut grow out and I began to turn up
the collar of my ski jacket. I spent most of my time with Casper, but
in spite of him, as the pale abbreviated days wore on, I found myself
growing more and more at ease with the idea of Maki Duryea.

She was still foreign, still exotic, still the new kid and worse,
much worse, the whole business complicated by the matter of her
skin color and her hair and the black unblinking depths of her eyes,
but she was there just like the rest of us and after a while it seemed
as if she'd always been there. She was in the other section, but I saw
her on the playground, in the hallway, saw her waiting on line in the
cafeteria with a tray in her hands or struggling up the steps of the
school bus in a knit hat and mittens no different from what the other
girls wore. I didn't have much to say to any of the girls really, but I
suppose I must have said things to her in passing, and once, coming
off the playground late, I found myself wedged up against her on the
crowded school bus. And then there was the time the dancing
teacher, with a casual flick of her wrist, paired me off with her.

Everything about dancing was excruciating. It was not kickball,
it was not basketball or bombardment. The potential for embarrass-
ment was incalculable. We were restless and bored, the gymnasium
was overheated against the sleet that rattled at the windows, and the
girls, entranced, wore peculiar little smiles as Mrs. Feldman demon-
strated the steps. The boys slouched against one adamantine wall,
poking one another, shuffling their feet and playing out an elaborate
ritual to demonstrate that none of this held the slightest interest for
them, for us, though it did, and we were nervous about it despite
ourselves. Alone, of all the two classes combined, Casper refused to
participate. Mrs. Feldman sent him to the principal's office without
so much as a second glance, chose partners arbitrarily for the

remainder of the class, and started up the ancient phonograph and the arcane scratchy records of songs no one knew and rhythms no one could follow, and before I was fully cognizant of what was happening I found myself clutching Maki Duryea's damp palm in my own while my arm lay like a dead thing across the small of her back. She was wearing a sweater thick enough for Arctic exploration and she was sweating in the choking humid jungle atmosphere of the gymnasium. I could smell her, but despite what Casper had said the heat of her body gave off a luxurious yeasty soporific odor that held me spellbound and upright through the droning eternity of the record.

The dance, the big dance that all this terpsichorean instruction was leading up to, was held on February 29, and Mrs. Feldman, in an evil twist of fate, decided to honor custom and have the girls invite the boys as their partners. We did perspective drawing in art class—great lopsided vistas of buildings and avenues dwindling in the distance—while the girls made up the invitations with strips of ribbon, construction paper, and paste. My mind was on basketball, ice fishing, the distant trembling vision of spring and summer, and liberation from Mrs. Feldman, the gym and the cafeteria and all the rest, and I was surprised, though I shouldn't have been, when Maki's invitation arrived. I didn't want to go. My mother insisted. My father said nothing.

And then the telephone began to ring. My mother answered each call with quiet determination, immovable, unshakable, whispering into the phone, doodling on a pad, lifting the drink or a cigarette to her lips. I don't know what she said exactly, but she was talking to the other mothers, the mothers of sons who hadn't been invited to the dance by Maki Duryea, and she was explaining to them precisely how and why she could and would allow her son to go to the dance with a Negro. In later years, as the civil-rights movement arose and Malcolm X and Martin Luther King fell and the ghettoes burned, she never had much to say about it, but I could feel her passion then, on the telephone, in the cool insistent rasp of her voice.

I went to the dance with Maki Duryea. She wore a stiff organdy dress with short sleeves that left her looking awkward and underdressed and I wore a tie and sportcoat and arranged my hair for the occasion. I held her and I danced with her, though I didn't want to, though I snapped at her when she asked if I wanted a brownie and a cup of punch, though I looked with envy and longing to the streamer-draped corner where Casper alternately leered at me and punched Billy Bartro in the shoulder; I danced with her, but that was it, that was as far as I could go, and I didn't care if the snow was black and the dome blew off the reactor and Johnny Atom came and melted us all in our sleep.

It was a late spring and we tried to force it by inaugurating baseball season while the snow still lingered atop the dead yellow grass and the frozen dirt beneath it. We dug out balls and mitts and stood in the street in T-shirts, gooseflesh on our arms, shoulders quaking, a nimbus of crystallized breath suspended over our heads. Casper didn't play ball—foot, hand, base, or basket—and he stood hunched in his jacket, palming a cigarette and watching us out of his mocking gray eyes. I caught cold and then flu and stayed in bed a week. On the first of April I went trout fishing, a ritual of spring, but the day was gloomy and lowering, with a stiff wind and temperatures in the twenties. I cast a baited hook till my arm lost all sensation. The trout might as well have been extinct.

Since the time of the dance I'd had nothing to do with Maki Duryea. I wouldn't even look at her. If she'd suddenly exploded in flames on the playground or swelled up to the size of a dirigible I wouldn't have known. I'd taken a steady stream of abuse over the dance episode, and I was angry and embarrassed. For a full month afterward I was the object of an accelerated program of ear snapping and head knuckling, the target of spitballs and wads of lined notebook paper with crude hearts scrawled across their rumpled interiors, but we were innocent then, and no one used the epithets we would later learn, the language of hate and exclusion. They turned on me because I had taken Maki Duryea to the dance—or rather, because I had allowed her to take me—and because she was different and their parents disapproved in a way they couldn't yet define. I resented her for it, and I resented my mother too.

And so, when the rumors first began to surface, I took a kind of guilty satisfaction in them. There had been trouble at Maki's house. Vandals—and the very term gave me a perverse thrill—vandals had spray-painted racial slurs on the glistening black surface of their macadam driveway. My mother was incensed. She took her drink and her cigarettes and huddled over the phone. She even formed a committee of two with Casper's mother (who was one of the few who hadn't phoned over the dance invitation), and they met a time or two in Casper's living room to drink a clear liquid in high-stemmed glasses, tap their cigarettes over ashtrays, and lament the sad state of the community, the development, the town, the country, the world itself.

While our mothers were wringing their hands and buzzing at one another in their rasping secretive voices, Casper took me aside and showed me a copy of the local newspaper, flung on the lawn not five minutes earlier by Morty Solomon as he weaved up the street on his bicycle. I didn't read newspapers. I didn't read books. I didn't read anything. Casper forced it into my hands and there it was, the rumor made concrete: VANDALS STRIKE AGAIN. This time, a cross had been burned on the Duryea lawn. I looked up at Casper in amazement. I wanted to ask him what that meant, a cross—a cross was religious, wasn't it, and this didn't have anything to do with religion, did it?— but I felt insecure in my confusion and I held back.

"You know what we ought to do?" he said, watching me closely.

I was thinking of Maki Duryea, of her hair and her placid eyes, thinking of the leaping flames and the spray paint in the driveway. "What?"

"We ought to egg them."

"But—" I was going to ask how we could egg them if we didn't know who did it, but then I caught the startling perverse drift of what he was suggesting and in my astonishment I blurted, "But why?"

He shrugged, ducked his head, scuffed a foot on the carpet. We were in the hallway, by the telephone stand. I heard my mother's voice from the room beyond, though the door was closed and she was talking in a whisper. The voice of Casper's mother came right back at her in raspy collusion. Casper just stared at the closed door as if to say, *There, there's your answer.*

After a moment he said, "What's the matter—you afraid?"

I was twelve now, twelve and a half. How could anyone at that age admit to fear? "No," I said. "I'm not afraid."

The Duryea house lay outside the confines of the development. It was a rental house, two stories over a double garage in need of paint and shingles, and it sat on a steep rutted dirt road half a mile away. There were no streetlights along that unfinished road and the trees overhung it so that the deepest shadows grew deeper still beneath them. It was a warm, slick, humid night at the end of May, the sort of night that surprises you with its richness and intensity, smells heightened, sounds muffled, lights blurred to indistinction. When we left Casper's it was drizzling.

Casper bought the eggs, two dozen, at the corner store out on the highway. His parents were rich—rich compared to mine, at any rate—and he always seemed to have money. The storekeeper was a tragic-looking man with purple rings of puffed flesh beneath his eyes and a spill of gut that was like an avalanche under the smeared white front of his apron. Casper slipped two cigars into his pocket while I distracted the man with a question about the chocolate milk—did it come in a smaller size?

As we started up the dirt road, eggs in hand, Casper was strangely silent. When a dog barked from the driveway of a darkened house he clutched my arm, and a moment later, when a car turned into the street, he pulled me into the bushes and crouched there, breathing hard, till the headlights faded away. "Maki Duryea," he whispered, chanting it as he'd chanted it a hundred times before, "Maki Duryea, Maki Duryea." My heart was hammering. I didn't want to do this. I didn't know why I was doing it, didn't yet realize that the whole purpose of the exercise was to invert our parents' values, trash them, grind them into the dirt, and that all ethical considerations were null in the face of that ancient imperative. I was a freedom fighter. The eggs were hand grenades. I clutched them to my chest.

We hid ourselves in the wild tangle of shrubs gone to seed outside the house and watched the steady pale lighted windows for movement. My hair hung limp with the drizzle. Casper squatted over his ankles and fingered his box of eggs. I could barely make him out. At one point a figure passed in front of the window—I saw the hair, the mat of it, the sheen—and it might have been Maki, but I wasn't sure. It could have been her mother. Or her sister or aunt or grandmother—it could have been anybody. Finally, when I was as tired of crouching there in the bushes as I've ever been tired of being anywhere, even the dentist's, the lights flicked off. Or no, they didn't just flick off—they exploded in darkness and the black torrent of the night rushed in to engulf the house.

Casper rose to his feet. I heard him fumbling with his cardboard carton of eggs. We didn't speak—speech would have been superfluous. I rose too. My eggs, palpable, smooth, fit the palm of my hand as if they'd been designed for it. I raised my arm—baseball, football, basketball—and Casper stirred beside me. The familiar motion, the rush of air: I will never forget the sound of that first egg loosing itself against the front of the house, a wetness there, a softness, the birth of something. No weapon, but a weapon all the same.

The summer sustained me. Hot, unfettered, endless. On the first day of vacation I perched in an apple tree at the end of the cul-de-sac that bordered the development and contemplated the expanse of time and pleasure before me, and then it was fall and I was in junior high. Maki Duryea had moved. I'd heard as much from Casper, and one afternoon, at the end of summer, I hiked up that long rutted dirt road to investigate. The house stood empty. I climbed the ridge behind it to peer in through the naked windows and make sure. Bare floors stretched to bare walls.

And then, in the confusion of the big parking lot at the junior high where fifty buses deposited the graduates of a dozen elementary schools, where I felt lost and out of place and shackled in a plaid long-sleeved shirt new that morning from the plastic wrapping, I saw her. She sprang down from another bus in a cascade of churning legs and arms and anxious faces, a bookbag slung over one shoulder, hair ironed to her waist. I couldn't move. She looked up then and saw me and she smiled. Then she was gone.

That night, as I slapped a hard black ball against the side of the house, thinking nothing, I caught a faint electrifying whiff of a forgotten scent on the air, and there he was, the fog man, rattling by the house in his open jeep. My bike lay waiting at the curb and my first impulse was to leap for it, but I held off. There was something different here, something I couldn't quite place at first. And then I saw what it was: the fog man was wearing a mask, a gas mask, the sort of thing you saw in war movies. He'd collected the usual escort of knee-pumping neighborhood kids by the time he'd made his second pass down the street in front of our house, and I'd moved to the curb now to study this phenomenon, this subtle alteration in the texture of things. He looked different in the mask, sinister somehow, and his eyes seemed to glitter.

The fog obliterated the houses across from me, the wheeling children vanished, the low black roiling clouds melted toward me across the perfect sweep of the lawn. And then, before I knew what I was doing, I was on my bike with the rest of them, chasing the fog man through the mist, chasing him as if my life depended on it.

(1989)

RARA AVIS

It looked like a woman or a girl perched there on the roof of the furniture store, wings folded like a shawl, long legs naked and exposed beneath a skirt of jagged feathers the color of sepia. The sun was pale, poised at equinox. There was the slightest breeze. We stood there, thirty or forty of us, gaping up at the big motionless bird as if we expected it to talk, as if it weren't a bird at all but a plastic replica with a speaker concealed in its mouth. Sidor's Furniture, it would squawk, love seats and three-piece sectionals.

I was twelve. I'd been banging a handball against the side of the store when a man in a Studebaker suddenly swerved into the parking lot, slammed on his brakes, and slid out of the driver's seat as if mesmerized. His head was tilted back, and he was shading his eyes, squinting to focus on something at the level of the roof. This was odd. Sidor's roof—a flat glaring expanse of crushed stone and tar relieved only by the neon characters that irradiated the proprietor's name—was no architectural wonder. What could be so captivating? I pocketed the handball and ambled round to the front of the store. Then I looked up.

There it was: stark and anomalous, a relic of a time before shopping centers, tract houses, gas stations and landfills, a thing of swamps and tidal flats, of ooze, fetid water, and rich black festering muck. In the context of the minutely ordered universe of suburbia, it was startling, as unexpected as a downed meteor or the carcass of a woolly mammoth. I shouted out, whooped with surprise and sudden joy.

Already people were gathering. Mrs. Novak, all three hundred pounds of her, was lumbering across the lot from her house on the corner, a look of bewilderment creasing her heavy jowls. Robbie Matechik wheeled up on his bike, a pair of girls emerged from the rear of the store with jump ropes, an old man in baggy trousers struggled with a bag of groceries. Two more cars pulled in, and a third stopped out on the highway. Hopper, Moe, Jennings, Davidson, Sebesta: the news echoed through the neighborhood as if relayed by tribal drums, and people dropped rakes, edgers, pruning shears, and came running. Michael Donadio, sixteen years old and a heartthrob at the local high school, was pumping gas at the station up the block. He left the nozzle in the customer's tank, jumped the fence, and started across the blacktop, weaving under his pompadour. The customer followed him.

At its height, there must have been fifty people gathered there in front of Sidor's, shading their eyes and gazing up expectantly, as if the bird were the opening act of a musical comedy or an ingenious new type of vending machine. The mood was jocular, festive even. Sidor appeared at the door of his shop with two stockboys, gazed up at the bird for a minute, and then clapped his hands twice, as if he were shooing pigeons. The bird remained motionless, cast in wax. Sidor, a fleshless old man with a monk's tonsure and liver-spotted hands, shrugged his shoulders and mugged for the crowd. We all laughed. Then he ducked into the store and emerged with an end table, a lamp, a footstool, motioned to the stockboys, and had them haul out a sofa and an armchair. Finally he scrawled BIRD WATCHER'S SPECIAL on a strip of cardboard and taped it to the window. People laughed and shook their heads. "Hey, Sidor," Albert Moe's father shouted, "where'd you get that thing—the Bronx Zoo?"

I couldn't keep still. I danced round the fringe of the crowd, tugging at sleeves and skirts, shouting out that I'd seen the bird first—which wasn't strictly true, but I felt proprietary about this strange and wonderful creature, the cynosure of an otherwise pedestrian Saturday afternoon. Had I seen it in the air? people asked. Had it moved? I was tempted to lie, to tell them I'd spotted it over the school, the firehouse, the used-car lot, a hovering shadow, wings spread wider than the hood of a Cadillac, but I couldn't. "No," I said, quiet suddenly. I glanced up and saw my father in the back of the crowd, standing close to Mrs. Schlecta and whispering something in her ear. Her lips were wet. I didn't know where my mother was. At the far end of the lot a girl in a college sweater was leaning against the fender of a convertible while her boyfriend pressed himself against her as if he wanted to dance.

Six weeks earlier, at night, the community had come together as it came together now, but there had been no sense of magic or festivity about the occasion. The Novaks, Donadios, Schlectas, and the rest—they gathered to watch an abandoned house go up in flames. I didn't dance round the crowd that night. I stood beside my father, leaned against him, the acrid, unforgiving stink of the smoke almost drowned in the elemental odor of his sweat, the odor of armpit and crotch and secret hair, the sematic animal scent of him that had always repelled me—until that moment. Janine McCarty's mother was shrieking. Ragged and torn, her voice clawed at the starless night, the leaping flames. On the front lawn, just as they backed the ambulance in and the crowd parted, I caught a glimpse of Janine, lying there in the grass. Every face was shouting. The glare of the fire tore disordered lines across people's eyes and dug furrows in their cheeks.

There was a noise to that fire, a killing noise, steady and implacable. The flames were like the waves at Coney Island—ghost waves, insubstantial, yellow and red rather than green, but waves all the same. They rolled across the foundation, spat from the windows, beat at the roof. Wayne Sanders was white-faced. He was a tough guy, two years older than I but held back in school because of mental sloth and recalcitrance. Police and firemen and wild-eyed neighborhood men nosed round him, excited, like hounds. Even then, in the grip of confusion and clashing voices, safe at my father's side, I knew what they wanted to know. It was the same thing my father demanded of me whenever he caught me—in fact or by report—emerging from the deserted, vandalized, and crumbling house: What were you doing in there?

He couldn't know.

Spires, parapets, derelict staircases, closets that opened on closets, the place was magnetic, vestige of an age before the neat rows of ranches and Cape Cods that lined both sides of the block. Plaster pulled back from the ceilings to reveal slats like ribs, glass pebbled the floors, the walls were paisleyed with aerosol obscenities. There were bats in the basement, rats and mice in the hallways. The house breathed death and freedom. I went there whenever I could. I heaved my interdicted knife end-over-end at the lintels and peeling cupboards, I lit cigarettes and hung them from my lower lip, I studied scraps of pornographic magazines with a fever beating through my body. Two days before the fire I was there with Wayne Sanders and Janine. They were holding hands. He had a switchblade, stiff and cold as an icicle. He gave me Ex-Lax and told me it was chocolate. Janine giggled. He shuffled a deck of battered playing cards and showed me one at a time the murky photos imprinted on them. My throat went dry with guilt.

After the fire I went to church. In the confessional the priest asked me if I practiced self-pollution. The words were formal, unfamiliar, but I knew what he meant. So, I thought, kneeling there in the dark, crushed with shame, there's a name for it. I looked at the shadowy grille, looked toward the source of the soothing voice of absolution, the voice of forgiveness and hope, and I lied. "No," I whispered.

And then there was the bird.

It never moved, not once, through all the commotion at its feet, through all the noise and confusion, all the speculation regarding its needs, condition, origin, species: it never moved. It was a statue, eyes unblinking, only the wind-rustled feathers giving it away for flesh and blood, for living bird. "It's a crane," somebody said. "No, no, it's a herring—a blue herring." Someone else thought it was an eagle. My father later confided that he believed it was a stork.

"Is it sick, do you think?" Mrs. Novak said.

"Maybe it's broke its wing."

"It's a female," someone insisted. "She's getting ready to lay her eggs."

I looked around and was surprised to see that the crowd had thinned considerably. The girl in the college sweater was gone, Michael Donadio was back across the street pumping gas, the man in the Studebaker had driven off. I scanned the crowd for my father: he'd gone home, I guessed. Mrs. Schlecta had disappeared too, and I could see the great bulk of Mrs. Novak receding into her house on the corner like a sea lion vanishing into a swell. After a while Sidor took his lamp and end table back into the store.

One of the older guys had a rake. He heaved it straight up like a javelin, as high as the roof of the store, and then watched it slam down on the pavement. The bird never flinched. People lit cigarettes, shuffled their feet. They began to drift off, one by one. When I looked around again there were only eight of us left, six kids and two men I didn't recognize. The women and girls, more easily bored or perhaps less interested to begin with, had gone home to gas ranges and hopscotch squares: I could see a few of the girls in the distance, on the swings in front of the school, tiny, their skirts rippling like flags.

I waited. I wanted the bird to flap its wings, blink an eye, shift a foot; I wanted it desperately, wanted it more than anything I had ever wanted. Perched there at the lip of the roof, its feet clutching the drainpipe as if welded to it, the bird was a coil of possibility, a muscle relaxed against the moment of tension. Yes, it was magnificent, even in repose. And, yes, I could stare at it, examine its every line, from its knobbed knees to the cropped feathers at the back of its head, I could absorb it, become it, look out from its unblinking yellow eyes on the street grown quiet and the sun sinking behind the gas station. Yes, but that wasn't enough. I had to see it in flight, had to see the great impossible wings beating in the air, had to see it transposed into its native element.

Suddenly the wind came up—a gust that raked at our hair and scattered refuse across the parking lot—and the bird's feathers lifted like a petticoat. It was then that I understood. Secret, raw, red and wet, the wound flashed just above the juncture of the legs before the wind died and the feathers fell back in place.

I turned and looked past the neighborhood kids—my play-mates—at the two men, the strangers. They were lean and seedy, unshaven, slouching behind the brims of their hats. One of them was chewing a toothpick. I caught their eyes: they'd seen it too.

I threw the first stone.

(1981)

THE CHAMP

Angelo D. was training hard. This challenger, Kid Gullet, would be no pushover. In fact, the Kid hit him right where he lived: he was worried. He'd been champ for thirty-seven years and all that time his records had stood like Mount Rushmore—and now this Kid was eating them up. Fretful, he pushed his plate away.

"But Angelo, you ain't done already?" His trainer, Spider Decoud, was all over him. "That's what—a piddling hundred and some–odd flapjacks and seven quarts a milk?"

"He's onto me, Spider. He found out about the ulcer and now he's going to hit me with enchiladas and shrimp in cocktail sauce."

"Don't fret it, Killer. We'll get him with the starches and heavy syrups. He's just a kid, twenty-two. What does he know about eating? Look, get up and walk it off and we'll do a kidney and kipper course, okay? And then maybe four or five dozen poached eggs. C'mon, Champ, lift that fork. You want to hold on to the title or not?"

First it was pickled eggs. Eighty-three pickled eggs in an hour and a half. The record had stood since 1941. They said it was like DiMaggio's consecutive-game hitting streak: unapproachable. A world apart. But then, just three months ago, Angelo had picked up the morning paper and found himself unforked: a man who went by the name of Kid Gullet had put down 108 of them. In the following weeks Angelo had seen his records toppled like a string of dominoes: gherkins, pullets, persimmons, oysters, pretzels, peanuts, scalloped potatoes, feta cheese, smelts, Girl Scout cookies. At the Rendezvous Room in Honolulu the Kid bolted 12,000 macadamia nuts and 67 bananas in less than an hour. During a Cubs–Phillies game at Wrigley Field he put away 43 hot dogs—with buns—and 112 Cokes. In Orkney it was legs of lamb; in Frankfurt, Emmentaler and schnitzel; in Kiev, pirogen. He was irrepressible. In Stelton, New Jersey, he finished off 6 gallons of borscht and 93 four-ounce jars of gefilte fish while sitting atop a flagpole. The press ate it up.

Toward the end of the New Jersey session a reporter from ABC Sports swung a boom mike up to where the Kid sat on his eminence, chewing the last of the gefilte fish. "What are your plans for the future, Kid?" shouted the newsman.

"I'm after the Big One," the Kid replied.

"Angelo D.?"

The camera zoomed in, the Kid grinned.

> *"Capocollo, chili and curry,*
> *Big Man, you better start to worry."*

Angelo was rattled. He gave up the morning paper and banned the use of the Kid's name around the Training Table. Kid Gullet: every time he heard those three syllables his stomach clenched. Now he lay on the bed, the powerful digestive machinery tearing away at breakfast, a bag of peanuts in his hand, his mind sifting through the tough bouts and spectacular triumphs of the past. There was Beau Riviere from Baton Rouge, who nearly choked him on deep-fried mud puppies, and Pinky Luzinski from Pittsburgh, who could gulp down 300 raw eggs and then crunch up the shells as if they were potato chips. Or the Japanese sumo wrestler who swallowed marbles by the fistful and throve on sashimi in a fiery mustard sauce. He'd beaten them all, because he had grit and determination and talent—and he would beat this kid too. Angelo sat up and roared: "I'm still the champ!"

The door cracked open. It was Decoud. "That's the spirit, Killer. Remember D. D. Peloris, Max Manger, Bozo Miller, Spoonbill Rizzo? Bums. All of them. You beat 'em, Champ."

"Yeah!" Angelo bellowed. "And I'm going to flatten this Gullet too."

"That's the ticket: leave him gasping for Bromo."

"They'll be pumping his stomach when I'm through with him."

Out in L.A. the Kid was taking on Turk Harris, number one contender for the heavyweight crown. The Kid's style was Tabasco and Worcestershire; Harris was a mashed-potato and creamed-corn man—a trencherman of the old school. Like Angelo D.

Harris opened with a one-two combination of rice and kidney beans; the Kid countered with cocktail onions and capers. Then Harris hit him with baklava—400 two-inch squares of it. The Kid gobbled them like hors d'oeuvres, came back with chiles rellenos and asparagus vinaigrette. He KO'd Harris in the middle of the fourth round. After the bout he stood in a circle of jabbing microphones, flashing lights. "I got one thing to say," he shouted. "And if you're out there, Big Man, you better take heed:

> *I'm going to float like a parfait,*
> *Sting like a tamale.*
> *Big Man, you'll hit the floor,*
> *In four."*

At the preliminary weigh-in for the title bout the Kid showed up on roller skates in a silver lamé jumpsuit. He looked like something off the launching pad at Cape Canaveral. Angelo, in his coal-bucket trousers and suspenders, could have been mistaken for an aging barber or a boccie player strayed in from the park.

The Kid had a gallon jar of hot cherry peppers under his arm. He wheeled up to the Champ, bolted six or seven in quick succession, and then held one out to him by the stem. "Care for an appetizer, Pops?" Angelo declined, his face dour and white, the big fleshy nostrils heaving like a stallion's. Then the photographers posed the two, belly to belly. In the photograph, which appeared on the front page of the paper the following morning, Angelo D. looked like an advertisement for heartburn.

There was an SRO crowd at the Garden for the title bout. Scalpers were getting two hundred and up for tickets. ABC Sports was there, Colonel Sanders was there, Arthur Treacher, Julia Child, James Beard, Ronald McDonald, Mamma Leone. It was the Trenching Event of the Century.

Spider Decoud and the Kid's manager had inspected the ring and found the arrangements to their satisfaction—each man had a table, stool, stack of plates and cutlery. Linen napkins, a pitcher of water. It would be a fourteen-round affair, each round going ten minutes with a sixty-second bell break. The contestants would name their dishes for alternate rounds, the Kid, as challenger, leading off.

A hush fell over the crowd. And then the chant, rolling from back to front like breakers washing the beach: GULLET, GULLET, GULLET! There he was, the Kid, sweeping down the aisle like a born champion in his cinnamon-red robe with the silver letters across the abdomen. He stepped into the ring, clasped his hands, and shook them over his head. The crowd roared like rock faces slipping deep beneath the earth. Then he did a couple of deep knee bends and sat down on his stool. At that moment Angelo shuffled out from the opposite end of the arena, stern, grim, raging, the tight curls at the back of his neck standing out like the tail feathers of an albatross, his barren dome ghostly under the klieg lights, the celebrated paunch swelling beneath his opalescent robe like a fat wad of butterball turkeys. The crowd went mad. They shrieked, hooted and whistled, women kissed the hem of his gown, men reached out to pat his bulge. ANGELO! He stepped into the ring and took his seat as the big black mike descended from the ceiling.

The announcer, in double lapels and bow tie, shouted over the roar, "Ladies and Gentlemen—" while Angelo glared at the Kid, blood in his eye. He was choked with a primordial competitive fury, mad as a kamikaze, deranged with hunger. Two days earlier Decoud had lured him into a deserted meat locker and bolted the door—and then for the entire forty-eight hours had projected pornographic food films on the wall. Fleshy wet lips closing on éclairs, zoom shots of masticating teeth, gulping throats, probing tongues, children innocently sucking at Tootsie Roll pops—it was obscene, titillating, maddening. And through it all a panting soundtrack composed of grunts and sighs and the smack of lips. Angelo D. climbed into the ring a desperate man. But even money nonetheless. The Kid gloated in his corner.

"At this table, in the crimson trunks," bellowed the announcer, "standing six foot two inches tall and weighing in at three hundred and seventy-seven pounds . . . is the challenger, Kid Gullet!" A cheer went up, deafening. The announcer pointed to Angelo. "And at this table, in the pearly trunks and standing five foot seven and a half inches tall and weighing in at three hundred and twenty-three pounds," he bawled, his voice rumbling like a cordon of cement trucks, "is the Heavyweight Champion of the World . . . Angelo D.!" Another cheer, perhaps even louder. Then the referee took over. He had the contestants step to the center of the ring, the exposed flesh of their chests and bellies like a pair of avalanches, while he asked if each was acquainted with the rules. The Kid grinned like a shark. "All right then," the ref said, "touch midriffs and come out eating."

The bell rang for Round One. The Kid opened with Szechwan hot and sour soup, three gallons. He lifted the tureen to his lips and slapped it down empty. The Champ followed suit, his face aflame, sweat breaking out on his forehead. He paused three times, and when finally he set the tureen down he snatched up the water pitcher and drained it at a gulp while the crowd booed and Decoud yelled from the corner: "Lay off the water or you'll bloat up like a blowfish!"

Angelo retaliated with clams on the half shell in Round Two: 512 in ten minutes. But the Kid kept pace with him—and as if that weren't enough, he sprinkled his own portion with cayenne pepper and Tabasco. The crowd loved it. They gagged on their hot dogs, pelted the contestants with plastic cups and peanut shells, gnawed at the backs of their seats. Angelo looked up at the Kid's powerful jaws, the lips stained with Tabasco, and began to feel queasy.

The Kid staggered him with lamb curry in the next round. The crowd was on its feet, the Champ's face was green, the fork motionless in his hand, the ref counting down. Decoud twisting the towel in his fists—when suddenly the bell sounded and the Champ collapsed on the table. Decoud leaped into the ring, chafed Angelo's abdomen, sponged his face. "Hang in there, Champ," he said, "and come back hard with the carbohydrates."

Angelo struck back with potato gnocchi in Round Four; the Kid countered with Kentucky burgoo. They traded blows through the next several rounds, the Champ scoring with Nesselrode pie, fettuccine Alfredo, and poi, the Kid lashing back with jambalaya, shrimp creole, and herring in horseradish sauce.

After the bell ending Round Eleven, the bout had to be held up momentarily because of a disturbance in the audience. Two men, thin as tapers and with beards like Spanish moss, had leaped into the ring waving posters that read REMEMBER BIAFRA. The Kid started up from his table and pinned one of them to the mat, while security guards nabbed the other. The Champ sat immobile on his stool, eyes tearing from the horseradish sauce, his fist clenched round the handle of the water pitcher. When the ring was cleared the bell rang for Round Twelve.

It was the Champ's round all the way: sweet potato pie with butterscotch syrup and pralines. For the first time the Kid let up—toward the end of the round he dropped his fork and took a mandatory eight count. But he came back strong in the thirteenth with a savage combination of Texas wieners and sauce diable. The Champ staggered, went down once, twice, flung himself at the water pitcher while the Kid gorged like a machine, wiener after wiener, blithely lapping the hot sauce from his fingers and knuckles with an epicurean relish. Then Angelo's head fell to the table, his huge whiskered jowl mired in a pool of béchamel and butter. The fans sprang to their feet, feinting left and right, snapping their jaws and yabbering for the kill. The Champ's eyes fluttered open, the ref counted over him.

It was then that it happened. His vision blurring, Angelo gazed out into the crowd and focused suddenly on the stooped and wizened figure of an old woman in a black bonnet. Decoud stood at her elbow. Angelo lifted his head. "Ma?" he said. "Eat, Angelo, eat!" she called, her voice a whisper in the apocalyptic thunder of the crowd. "Clean your plate!"

"Nine!" howled the referee, and suddenly the Champ came to life, lashing into the sauce diable like a crocodile. He bolted wieners, sucked at his fingers, licked the plate. Some say his hands moved so fast that they defied the eye, a mere blur, slapstick in double time. Then the bell rang for the final round and Angelo announced his dish: "Gruel!" he roared. The Kid protested. "What kind of dish is that?" he whined. "Gruel? Whoever heard of gruel in a championship bout?" But gruel it was. The Champ lifted the bowl to his lips, pasty ropes of congealed porridge trailing down his chest; the crowd cheered, the Kid toyed with his spoon—and then it was over.

The referee stepped in, helped Angelo from the stool, and held his flaccid arm aloft. Angelo was plate-drunk, reeling. He looked out over the cheering mob, a welter of button heads like B in B mushrooms—or Swedish meatballs in a rich golden sauce. Then he gagged. "The winner," the ref was shouting, "and still champion, Angelo D.!"

(1977)

BEAT

Yeah, I was Beat. We were all Beat. Hell, I'm Beat now—is, was, and always will be. I mean, how do you stop? But this isn't about me— I'm nobody, really, just window-dressing on the whole mother of Bop freight-train-hopping holy higher than Tokay Beat trip into the heart of the American night. No, what I wanted to tell you about is Jack. And Neal and Allen and Bill and all the rest too, and how it all went down, because I was there, I was on the scene, and there was nobody Beater than me.

Picture this: seventeen years old, hair an unholy mess and a little loden-green beret perched up on top to keep it in place, eighty-three cents in my pocket, and a finger-greased copy of *The Subterraneans* in my rucksack along with a Charlie Parker disc with enough pops, scratches, and white noise worked into the grooves to fill out the soundtrack of a sci-fi flick, hitched all the way from Oxnard, California, and there I am on Jack's front porch in Northport, Long Island, December twenty-three, nineteen fifty-eight. It's cold. Bleak. The town full of paint-peeling old monster houses, gray and worn and just plain old, like the whole horse-blindered tired-out East Coast locked in its gloom from October to April with no time off for good behavior. I'm wearing three sweaters under my Levi's jacket and still I'm holding on to my ribs and I can feel the snot crusting round my nostrils and these mittens I bummed from an old lady at the Omaha bus station are stiff with it, and I knock, wondering if there's an officially cool way to knock, a hipster's way, a kind of secret Dharma Bums code-knock I don't know about.

Knock-knock. Knockata-knockata, knock-knock-knock.

My first surprise was in store: it wasn't Jack, the gone hep satori-seeking poet god of the rails and two-lane blacktop, who answered the door, but a big blocky old lady with a face like the bottom of a hiking boot. She was wearing a dress the size of something you'd drape over a car to keep the dust off it, and it was composed of a thousand little red and green triangles with gold trumpets and silver angels squeezed inside of them. She gave me the kind of look that could peel the tread off a recapped tire, the door held just ajar. I shuddered: she looked like somebody's mother.

My own mother was three thousand miles away and so square she was cubed; my dog, the one I'd had since childhood, was dead, flattened out by a big rig the week earlier; and I'd flunked English, History, Calculus, Art, Phys. Ed., Music, and Lunch. I wanted adventure, the life of the road, freewheeling chicks in berets and tea and bongos and long Benzedrine-inflected bullshit sessions that ran on into morning, I wanted Jack and everything he stood for, and here was this old lady. "Uh," I stammered, fighting to control my voice, which was just then deepening from the adolescent squeak I'd had to live with since consciousness had hit, "does, uh, Jack Kerouac live here, I mean, by any chance?"

"Go back where you came from," the old lady said. "My Jacky don't have time for no more of this nonsense." And that was it: she shut the door in my face.

My Jacky!

It came to me then: this was none other than Jack's mother, the Bop-nurturing freewheeling wild Madonna herself, the woman who'd raised up the guru and given him form, mother of us all. And she'd locked me out. I'd come three thousand miles, her Jacky was my Jack, and I was cold through to the bone, stone broke, scared, heartsick, and just about a lungful of O₂ away from throwing myself down in the slush and sobbing till somebody came out and shot me. I knocked again.

"Hey, Ma," I heard from somewhere deep inside the house, and it was like the rutting call of some dangerous beast, a muted angry threatening Bop-benny-and-jug-wine roar, the voice of the man himself, "what the hell is this, I'm trying to concentrate in here."

And then the old lady: "It ain't nothing, Jacky."

Knock-knock. Knockata-knockata, knock-knock-knock. I paradiddled that door, knocked it and socked it, beat on it like it was the bald flat-topped dome of my uptight pencil-pushing drudge of a bourgeois father himself, or maybe Mr. Detwinder, the principal at Oxnard High. I knocked till my knuckles bled, a virtuoso of knocking, so caught up in the rhythm and energy of it that it took me a minute to realize the door was open and Jack himself standing there in the doorway. He looked the way Belmondo tried to look in *Breathless*, loose and cool in a rumpled T-shirt and jeans, with a smoke in one hand, a bottle of muscatel in the other.

I stopped knocking. My mouth fell open and the snot froze in my nostrils. "Jack Kerouac," I said.

He let a grin slide down one side of his mouth and back up the other. "Nobody else," he said.

The wind shot down my collar, I caught a glimpse of colored lights blinking on and off in the room behind him, and suddenly it was all gushing out of me like something I'd been chewing over and digesting all my life: "I hitched all the way from Oxnard and my name's Wallace Pinto but you can call me Buzz and I just wanted to say, I just wanted to tell you—"

"Yeah, yeah, I know," he said, waving a hand in dismissal, and he seemed unsteady on his muscatel-impaired feet, the smoke curling up to snatch at his cracked blue squinting eyes, the words slow on his lips, heavy, weighted and freighted with the deep everlasting bardic wisdom of the road, the cathouse, and the seaman's bar, "but I tell you, kid, you keep drumming on the door like that you're going to end up in the hospital"—a pause—"or maybe a jazz combo." I just stood there in a kind of trance until I felt his hand—his Dharma Bum Subterranean On the Road Bop-master's gone Mexican-chick-digging hand—take hold of my shoulder and tug me forward, over the threshold and into the house. "You ever been introduced to a true and veritable set of tight-skinned bongos?" he asked, throwing an arm over my shoulder as the door slammed behind us.

Two hours later we were sitting there in the front room by this totally gone Christmas tree bedecked with cherubim and little Christs and the like, indulging in a poor boy and a joint or two of Miss Green, my Charlie Parker record whizzing and popping on the record player and a whole big pile of red and green construction-paper strips growing at our feet. We were making a chain to drape over the Beatest tree you ever saw and the music was a cool breeze fluttering full of Yardbird breath and the smell of ambrosia and manna crept in from the kitchen where Mémère, the Beat Madonna herself, was cooking up some first-rate mouthwatering Canuck-style two-days-before-Christmas chow. I hadn't eaten since New Jersey, the morning before, and that was only some pretty piss-poor diner hash fries and a runny solitary egg, and I was cutting up little strips of colored paper and pasting them in little circles as Jack's chain grew and my head spun from the wine and the weed.

That big old lady in the Christmas dress just kind of vanished and the food appeared, and we ate, Jack and I, side by side, left our Beat plates on the sofa, threw our chain on the tree, and were just pawing through the coats in the front hallway for another poor boy of sweet Tokay wine when there was a knock at the door. This knock wasn't like my knock. Not at all. This was a delicate knock, understated and minimalistic, but with a whole deep continent of passion and expectation implicit in it—in short, a feminine knock. "Well," Jack said, his face lit with the Beatest joy at discovering the slim vessel of a pint bottle in the inside pocket of his seaman's pea coat, "aren't you going to answer it?"

"Me?" I said, grinning my Beatest grin. I was in, I was part of it all, I was Jack's confidant and compatriot, and we were in the front hallway of his pad in Northport, Long Island, a fine hot steaming mother-of-Jack-prepared meal in our gone Beat guts, and he was asking me to answer the door, me, seventeen years old and nobody. "You mean it?" and my grin widened till I could feel the creeping seeping East Coast chill all the way back to my suburban-dentist-filled molars.

Jack, uncapping, tipping back, passing the bottle: "That's a chick knock, Buzz."

Me: "I love chicks."

Jack: "A gone lovely spring flower of a beret-wearing flipped long-legged coltish retroussé-nosed and run-away-from-home-to-big-Jack-Kerouac chick knock."

Me: "I am crazy for gone lovely spring flower beret-wearing flipped long-legged coltish retroussé-nosed run-away-from-home-to-big-Jack-Kerouac chicks."

Jack: "Then answer it."

I pulled open the door and there she was, all the above and more, sixteen years old with big ungulate eyes and Mary Travers hair. She gave me a gaping openmouthed look, taking in my loden-green beret, the frizzed wildness of my hair sticking out from under it, my Beat Levi's jacket and jeans, and my tea-reddened joyous hitching-all-the-way-from-Oxnard eyes. "I was looking for Jack," she said, and her voice was cracked and scratchy and low. She dropped her gaze.

I looked to Jack, who stood behind me, out of her line of vision, and asked a question with my eyebrows. Jack gave me his hooded smoldering dust-jacket-from-hell look, then stepped forward, took the poor boy from me, and loomed over the now-eye-lifting chick and chucked her chin with a gone Beat curling index finger. "Coochie-coochie-coo," he said.

Her name was Ricky Keen (Richarda Kinkowski, actually, but that's how she introduced herself), she'd hitchhiked all the way down from Plattsburgh, and she was as full of hero-worship and inarticulate praise as I was. "Dean Moriarty," she said at the end of a long rambling speech that alluded to nearly every line Jack had written and half the Zoot Sims catalogue, "he's the coolest. I mean, that's who I want to make babies with, absolutely."

There we were, standing in the front hallway listening to this crack-voiced ungulate-eyed long gone Beat-haired sixteen-year-old chick talk about making babies with Charlie Parker riffing in the background and the Christmas lights winking on and off and it was strange and poignant. All I could say was "Wow," over and over, but Jack knew just what to do. He threw one arm over my shoulder and the other over the chick's and he thrust his already-bloating and booze-inflamed but quintessentially Beat face into ours and said, low and rumbly, "What we need, the three of us hepsters, cats and chicks alike, is a consciousness-raising all-night bull session at the indubitable pinnacle of all neighborhood Bodhisattva centers and bar and grills, the Peroration Pub, or, as the fellaheen know it, Ziggy's Clam House. What do you say?"

What did we say? We were speechless—stunned, amazed, moved almost to tears. The man himself, he who had practically invented the mug, the jug, and the highball and lifted the art of getting sloshed to its Beat apotheosis, was asking us, the skinny underage bedraggled runaways, to go out on the town for a night of wild and prodigious Kerouackian drinking. All I could manage was a nod of assent, Ricky Keen said, "Yeah, sure, like wow," and then we were out in the frozen rain, the three of us, the streets all crusted with ugly East Coast ice, Ricky on one side of Jack, me on the other, Jack's arms uniting us. We tasted freedom on those frozen streets, passing the bottle, our minds elevated and feverish with the fat spike of Mary Jane that appeared magically between Jack's thumb and forefinger and the little strips of Benzedrine-soaked felt he made us swallow like a sacrament. The wind sang a dirge. Ice clattered down out of the sky. We didn't care. We walked eight blocks, our Beat jackets open to the elements, and we didn't feel a thing.

Ziggy's Clam House loomed up out of the frozen black wastes of the Long Island night like a ziggurat, a holy temple of Beat enlightenment and deep soul truths, lit only by the thin neon braids of the beer signs in the windows. Ricky Keen giggled. My heart was pounding against my ribs. I'd never been in a bar before and I was afraid I'd make an ass of myself. But not to worry: we were with Jack, and Jack never hesitated. He hit the door of Ziggy's Clam House like a fullback bursting through the line, the door lurched back on its hinges and embedded itself in the wall, and even as I clutched reflexively at the eighty-three cents in my pocket Jack stormed the bar with a roar: "Set up the house, barkeep, and all you sleepy fellaheen, the Beat Generation has arrived!"

I exchanged a glance with Ricky Keen. The place was as quiet as a mortuary, some kind of tacky Hawaiian design painted on the walls, a couple of plastic palms so deep in dust they might have been snowed on, and it was nearly as dark inside as out. The bartender, startled by Jack's joyous full-throated proclamation of Beat uplift and infectious Dionysian spirit, glanced up from the flickering blue trance of the TV like a man whose last stay of execution has just been denied. He was heavy in the jowls, favoring a dirty white dress shirt and a little bow tie pinned like a dead insect to his collar. He winced when Jack brought his Beat fist down on the countertop and boomed, "Some of everything for everybody!"

Ricky Keen and I followed in Jack's wake, lit by our proximity to the centrifuge of Beatdom and the wine, marijuana, and speed coursing through our gone adolescent veins. We blinked in the dim light and saw that the everybody Jack was referring to comprised a group of three: a sad mystical powerfully made-up cocktail waitress in a black tutu and fishnet stockings and a pair of crewcut Teamster types in blue workshirts and chinos. The larger of the two, a man with a face like a side of beef, squinted up briefly from his cigarette and growled. "Pipe down, asshole—can't you see we're trying to concentrate here?" Then the big rippled neck rotated and the head swung back round to refixate on the tube.

Up on the screen, which was perched between gallon jars of pickled eggs and Polish sausage, Red Skelton was mugging in a Santa Claus hat for all the dead vacant mindless living rooms of America, and I knew, with a deep sinking gulf of overwhelming un-Beat sadness, that my own triple-square parents, all the way out in Oxnard, were huddled round the console watching this same rubbery face go through its contortions and wondering where their pride and joy had got himself to. Ricky Keen might have been thinking along similar lines, so sad and stricken did she look at that moment, and I wanted to put my arms around her and stroke her hair and feel the heat of her Beat little lost body against my own. Only Jack seemed unaffected. "Beers all around," he insisted, tattooing the bar with his fist, and even before the bartender could heave himself up off his stool to comply Jack was waking up Benny Goodman on the jukebox and we were pooling our change as the Teamsters sat stoically beside their fresh Jack-bought beers and the cocktail waitress regarded us out of a pair of black staved-in eyes. Of course, Jack was broke and my eighty-three cents didn't take us far, but fortunately Ricky Keen produced a wad of crumpled dollar bills from a little purse tucked away in her boot and the beer flowed like bitter honey.

It was sometime during our third or fourth round that the burlier of the two Teamster types erupted from his barstool with the words *Communist* and *faggot* on his lips and flattened Jack, Ricky, and me beneath a windmill of punches, kicks, and elbow chops. We went down in a marijuana-weakened puddle, laughing like madmen, not even attempting to resist as the other Teamster, the bartender, and even the waitress joined in. Half a purple-bruised minute later the three of us were out on the icy street in a jumble of limbs and my hand accidentally wandered to Ricky Keen's hard little half-formed breast and for the first time I wondered what was going to become of me, and, more immediately, where I was going to spend the night.

But Jack, heroically Beat and muttering under his breath about squares and philistines, anticipated me. Staggering to his feet and reaching down a Tokay-cradling spontaneous-prose-generating railroad-callused hand first to Ricky and then to me, he said, "Fellow seekers and punching bags, the road to Enlightenment is a rocky one, but tonight, tonight you sleep with big Jack Kerouac."

I woke the next afternoon on the sofa in the living room of the pad Jack shared with his Mémère. The sofa was grueling terrain, pocked and scoured by random dips and high hard draft-buffeted plateaus, but my stringy impervious seventeen-year-old form had become one with it in a way that approached bliss. It was, after all, a sofa, and not the cramped front seat of an A & P produce truck or road-hopping Dodge, and it had the rugged book-thumbing late-night-crashing bongo-thumping joint-rolling aura of Jack to recommend and sanctify it. So what if my head was big as a weather balloon and the rest of me felt like so many pounds and ounces of beef jerky? So what if I was nauseated from cheap wine and tea and Benzedrine and my tongue was stuck like Velcro to the roof of my mouth and Ricky Keen was snoring on the floor instead of sharing the sofa with me? So what if Bing Crosby and Mario Lanza were blaring square Christmas carols from the radio in the kitchen and Jack's big hunkering soul of a mother maneuvered her shouldery bulk into the room every five seconds to give me a look of radiant hatred and motherly impatience? So what? I was at Jack's. Nirvana attained.

When finally I threw back the odd fuzzy Canuck-knitted detergent-smelling fully Beat afghan some kind soul—Jack?—had draped over me in the dim hours of the early morning, I became aware that

That was when Mémère came into the picture. She was steaming about something, really livid, her shoulders all hunched up and her face stamped with red-hot broiling uncontainable rage, but she served the flapjacks and we ate in Beat communion, fork-grabbing, syrup-pouring, and butter-smearing while Allen rhapsodized about the inner path and Jack poured wine. In retrospect, I should have been maybe a hair more attuned to Jack's mother and her moods, but I shoved flapjacks into my face, reveled in Beatdom, and ignored the piercing glances and rattling pans. Afterward we left our Beat plates where we dropped them and rushed into the living room to spin some sides and pound on the bongos while Allen danced a disheveled dance and blew into the wooden flute and Bill looked down the long tunnel of himself.

What can I say? The legends were gathered, we cut up the Benzedrine inhalers and swallowed the little supercharged strips of felt inside, feasted on Miss Green, and took a gone Beat hike to the liquor store for more wine and still more. By dark I was able to feel the wings of consciousness lift off my back and my memory of what came next is glorious but hazy. At some point—eight? nine?—I was aroused from my seventeen-year-old apprentice-Beat stupor by the sound of sniffling and choked-back sobs, and found myself looking up at the naked-but-for-a-seaman's-peacoat form of Ricky Keen. I seemed to be on the floor behind the couch, buried in a litter of doilies, antimacassars, and sheets of crumpled newspaper, the lights from the Christmas tree riding up the walls and Ricky Keen standing over me with her bare legs, heaving out chesty sobs and using the ends of her long gone hair to dab at the puddles of her eyes. "What?" I said. "What is it?" She swayed back and forth, rocking on her naked feet, and I couldn't help admiring her knees and the way her bare young hitchhiking thighs sprouted upward from them to disappear in the folds of the coat.

"It's Jack," she sobbed, the sweet rasp of her voice catching in her throat, and then she was behind the couch and kneeling like a supplicant over the jean-clad poles of my outstretched legs.

"Jack?" I repeated stupidly.

A moment of silence, deep and committed. There were no corny carols seeping from the radio in the kitchen, no wild tooth-baring jazz or Indian sutras roaring from the record player, there was no Allen, no Jack, no Mémère. If I'd been capable of sitting up and thrusting my head over the back of the sofa I would have seen that the room was deserted but for Bill, still locked in his comatose reverie. Ricky Keen sat on my knees. "Jack won't have me," she said in a voice so tiny I was hardly aware she was speaking at all. And then, with a pout: "He's drunk."

Jack wouldn't have her. I mulled fuzzily over this information, making slow drawn-out turtlelike connections while Ricky Keen sat on my knees with her golden eyes and Mary Travers hair, and finally I said to myself, If Jack won't have her, then who will? I didn't have a whole lot of experience along these lines—my adventures with the opposite sex had been limited to lingering dumbstruck classroom gazes and the odd double-feature grope—but I was willing to learn. And eager, oh yes.

"It's such a drag being a virgin," she breathed, unbuttoning the coat, and I sat up and took hold of her—clamped my panting per-spiring sex-crazed adolescent self to her, actually—and we kissed and throbbed and explored each other's anatomies in a drifting cloud of Beat bliss and gone holy rapture. I was lying there, much later, tin-gling with the quiet rush and thrill of it, Ricky breathing softly into the cradle of my right arm, when suddenly the front door flew back and the world's wildest heppest benny-crazed coast-to-coasting voice lit the room like a brushfire. I sat up. Groped for my pants. Cradled a startled Ricky head.

"Ho, ho, ho!" the voice boomed. "All you little boysies and girlsies been good? I been checkin' my list!"

I popped my head over the couch and there he was, cool and inexplicable. I couldn't believe my eyes: it was Neal. Neal escaped from San Quentin and dressed in a street-corner-Santa outfit, a bag full of booze, drugs, cigarettes, and canned hams slung over his back, his palms hammering invisible bongos in the air. "Come out, come out, wherever you are!" he cried, and broke down in a sea of giggles. "Gonna find out who's naughty and nice, yes indeed!"

At that moment Jack burst in from the kitchen, where he and Allen had been taking a little catnap over a jug of wine, and that was when the really wild times began, the back-thumping high-fiving jumping jiving tea-smoking scat-singing Beat revel of the ages. Ricky Keen came to life with a snort, wrapped the jacket round her, and stepped out from behind the couch like a Beat princess, I reached for the wine, Jack howled like a dog, and even Bill shifted his eyes round his head in a simulacrum of animacy. Neal couldn't stop talking and drinking and smoking, spinning round the room like a dervish, Allen shouted "Miles Davis!" and the record player came to life, and we were all dancing, even Bill, though he never left his chair.

That was the crowning moment of my life—I was Beat, finally and absolutely—and I wanted it to go on forever. And it could have, if it wasn't for Jack's mother, that square-shouldered fuming old woman in the Christmas dress. She was nowhere to be seen through all of this, and I'd forgotten about her in the crazed explosion of the moment—it wasn't till Jack began to break down that she materialized again.

It was around twelve or so. Jack got a little weepy, sang an a capella version of "Hark the Herald Angels Sing," and tried to talk us all into going to the midnight mass at St. Columbanus' church. Allen said he had no objection, except that he was Jewish, Neal derided the whole thing as the height of corny bourgeois sentimentality, Bill was having trouble moving his lips, and Ricky Keen said that she was Unitarian and didn't know if she could handle it. Jack, tears streaming down his face, turned to me. "Buzz," he said, and he had this wheedling crazed biggest-thing-in-the-world sort of edge to his voice, "Buzz, you're a good Catholic, I know you are—what do you say?"

All eyes focused on me. Silence rang suddenly through the house. I was three sheets to the wind, sloppy drunk, seventeen years old. Jack wanted to go to midnight mass, and it was up to me to say yea or nay. I just stood there, wondering how I was going to break the news to Jack that I was an atheist and that I hated God, Jesus, and my mother, who'd made me go to parochial school five days a week since I'd learned to walk and religious instruction on Sundays to boot. My mouth moved, but nothing came out.

Jack was trembling. A tic started in over his right eye. He clenched his fists. "Don't let me down, Buzz!" he roared, and when he started toward me Neal tried to stop him, but Jack flung him away as if he was nothing. "Midnight mass, Buzz, midnight!" he boomed, and he was standing right there in front of me, gone Beat crazy, and I could smell the booze on his stinking Beat breath. He dropped his voice then. "You'll rot in hell, Buzz," he hissed, "you'll rot." Allen reached for his arm, but Jack shook him off. I took a step back.

That was when Mémère appeared.

She swept into the room like something out of a Japanese monster flick, huge in her nightdress, big old Jack-mothery toes sticking out beneath it like sausages, and she went straight to the fireplace and snatched up the poker. "Out!" she screamed, the eyes sunk back in her head. "Get out of my house, you queers and convicts and drug addicts, and you"—she turned on me and Ricky—"you so-called fans and adulators, you're even worse. Go back where you came from and leave my Jacky in peace." She made as if to swing the poker at me and I reflexively ducked out of the way, but she brought it down across the lamp on the table instead. There was a flash, the lamp exploded, and she drew back and whipped the poker like a lariat over her head. "Out!" she shrieked, and the whole group, even Bill, edged toward the door.

Jack did nothing to stop her. He gave us his brooding lumber-jack Beat posing-on-the-fire-escape look, but there was something else to it, something new, and as I backpedaled out the door and into the grimy raw East Coast night, I saw what it was—the look of a mama's boy, pouty and spoiled. "Go home to your mothers, all of you," Mémère yelled, shaking the poker at us as we stood there drop-jawed on the dead brown ice-covered pelt of the lawn. "For god's sake," she sobbed, "it's Christmas!" And then the door slammed shut.

I was in shock. I looked at Bill, Allen, Neal, and they were as stunned as I was. And poor Ricky—all she had on was Jack's pea coat and I could see her tiny bare perfect-toed Beat chick feet freezing to the ground like twin ice sculptures. I reached up to adjust my beret and realized it wasn't there, and it was like I'd had the wind knocked out of me. "Jack!" I cried out suddenly, and my creaking adolescent voice turned it into a forlorn bleat. "Jack!" I cried, "Jack!" but the night closed round us and there was no answer.

What happened from there is a long story. But to make it short, I took Mémère's advice and went home to my mother, and by the time I got there Ricky had already missed her period. My mother didn't like it but the two of us moved into my boyhood room with the lame college pennants and dinosaur posters and whatnot on the walls for about a month, which is all we could stand, and then Ricky took her gone gorgeous Beat Madonna-of-the-streets little body off to an ultra-Beat one-room pad on the other end of town and I got a job as a brakeman on the Southern Pacific and she let me crash with her and that was that. We smoked tea and burned candles and incense and drank jug wine and made it till we damn near rubbed the skin off each other. The first four boys we named Jack, Neal, Allen, and Bill, though we never saw any of their namesakes again except Allen, at one of his poetry readings, but he made like he didn't know us. The first of the girls we named Gabrielle, for Jack's mother, and after that we seemed to kind of just lose track and name them for the month they were born, regardless of sex, and we wound up with two Junes—June the Male and June the Female—but it was no big thing.

Yeah, I was Beat, Beater than any of them—or just as Beat,

anyway. Looking back on it now, though, I mean after all these years and what with the mortgage payments and Ricky's detox and the kids with their college tuition and the way the woodworking shop over the garage burned down and how stinking closefisted petit-bourgeois before-the-revolution pigheaded cheap the railroad disability is, I wonder now if I'm not so much Beat anymore as just plain beat. But then, I couldn't even begin to find the words to describe it to you.

(1993)

GREASY LAKE

It's about a mile down on the dark side of Route 88.
                                    —Bruce Springsteen

There was a time when courtesy and winning ways went out of style, when it was good to be bad, when you cultivated decadence like a taste. We were all dangerous characters then. We wore torn-up leather jackets, slouched around with toothpicks in our mouths, sniffed glue and ether and what somebody claimed was cocaine. When we wheeled our parents' whining station wagons out into the street we left a patch of rubber half a block long. We drank gin and grape juice, Tango, Thunderbird, and Bali Hai. We were nineteen. We were bad. We read André Gide and struck elaborate poses to show that we didn't give a shit about anything. At night, we went up to Greasy Lake.

Through the center of town, up the strip, past the housing developments and shopping malls, streetlights giving way to the thin streaming illumination of the headlights, trees crowding the asphalt in a black unbroken wall: that was the way out to Greasy Lake. The Indians had called it Wakan, a reference to the clarity of its waters. Now it was fetid and murky, the mud banks glittering with broken glass and strewn with beer cans and the charred remains of bonfires. There was a single ravaged island a hundred yards from shore, so stripped of vegetation it looked as if the air force had strafed it. We went up to the lake because everyone went there, because we wanted to snuff the rich scent of possibility on the breeze, watch a girl take off her clothes and plunge into the festering murk, drink beer, smoke pot, howl at the stars, savor the incongruous full-throated roar of rock and roll against the primeval susurrus of frogs and crickets. This was nature.

I was there one night, late, in the company of two dangerous characters. Digby wore a gold star in his right ear and allowed his father to pay his tuition at Cornell; Jeff was thinking of quitting school to become a painter/musician/headshop proprietor. They were both expert in the social graces, quick with a sneer, able to manage a Ford with lousy shocks over a rutted and gutted blacktop road at eighty-five while rolling a joint as compact as a Tootsie Roll Pop stick. They could lounge against a bank of booming speakers and trade "man"s with the best of them or roll out across the dance floor as if their joints worked on bearings. They were slick and quick and they wore their mirror shades at breakfast and dinner, in the shower, in closets and caves. In short, they were bad.

I drove, Digby pounded the dashboard and shouted along with Toots & the Maytals while Jeff hung his head out the window and streaked the side of my mother's Bel Air with vomit. It was early June, the air soft as a hand on your cheek, the third night of summer vacation. The first two nights we'd been out till dawn, looking for something we never found. On this, the third night, we'd cruised the strip sixty-seven times, been in and out of every bar and club we could think of in a twenty-mile radius, stopped twice for bucket chicken and forty-cent hamburgers, debated going to a party at the house of a girl Jeff's sister knew, and chucked two dozen raw eggs at mailboxes and hitch-hikers. It was 2:00 A.M.; the bars were closing. There was nothing to do but take a bottle of lemon-flavored gin up to Greasy Lake.

The taillights of a single car winked at us as we swung into the dirt lot with its tufts of weed and washboard corrugations; '57 Chevy, mint, metallic blue. On the far side of the lot, like the exoskeleton of some gaunt chrome insect, a chopper leaned against its kickstand. And that was it for excitement: some junkie half-wit biker and a car freak pumping his girlfriend. Whatever it was we were looking for, we weren't about to find it at Greasy Lake. Not that night.

But then all of a sudden Digby was fighting for the wheel. "Hey, that's Tony Lovett's car! Hey!" he shouted, while I stabbed at the brake pedal and the Bel Air nosed up to the gleaming bumper of the parked Chevy. Digby leaned on the horn, laughing, and instructed me to put my brights on. I flicked on the brights. This was hilarious. A joke. Tony would experience premature withdrawal and expect to be confronted by grim-looking state troopers with flashlights. We hit the horn, strobed the lights, and then jumped out of the car to press our witty faces to Tony's windows; for all we knew we might even catch a glimpse of some little fox's tit, and then we could slap backs with red-faced Tony, roughhouse a little, and go on to new heights of adventure and daring.

The first mistake, the one that opened the whole floodgate, was losing my grip on the keys. In the excitement, leaping from the car with the gin in one hand and a roach clip in the other, I spilled them in the grass—in the dark, rank, mysterious nighttime grass of Greasy Lake. This was a tactical error, as damaging and irreversible in its way as Westmoreland's decision to dig in at Khe Sanh. I felt it like a jab of intuition, and I stopped there by the open door, peering vaguely into the night that puddled up round my feet.

The second mistake—and this was inextricably bound up with the first—was identifying the car as Tony Lovett's. Even before the very bad character in greasy jeans and engineer boots ripped out of the driver's door, I began to realize that this chrome blue was much lighter than the robin's-egg of Tony's car, and that Tony's car didn't have rear-mounted speakers. Judging from their expressions, Digby and Jeff were privately groping toward the same inevitable and unsettling conclusion as I was.

In any case, there was no reasoning with this bad greasy character—clearly he was a man of action. The first lusty Rockette's kick of his steel-toed boot caught me under the chin, chipped my favorite tooth, and left me sprawled in the dirt. Like a fool, I'd gone down on one knee to comb the stiff hacked grass for the keys, my mind making connections in the most dragged-out, testudineous way, knowing that things had gone wrong, that I was in a lot of trouble, and that the lost ignition key was my grail and my salvation. The three or four succeeding blows were mainly absorbed by my right buttock and the tough piece of bone at the base of my spine.

Meanwhile, Digby vaulted the kissing bumpers and delivered a savage kung-fu blow to the greasy character's collarbone. Digby had just finished a course in martial arts for phys-ed credit and had spent the better part of the past two nights telling us apocryphal tales of Bruce Lee types and of the raw power invested in lightning blows shot from coiled wrists, ankles, and elbows. The greasy character was unimpressed. He merely backed off a step, his face like a Toltec mask, and laid Digby out with a single whistling roundhouse blow . . . but by now Jeff had got into the act, and I was beginning to extricate myself from the dirt, a tinny compound of shock, rage, and impotence wadded in my throat.

Jeff was on the guy's back, biting at his ear. Digby was on the ground, cursing. I went for the tire iron I kept under the driver's seat. I kept it there because bad characters always keep tire irons under the driver's seat, for just such an occasion as this. Never mind that I hadn't been involved in a fight since sixth grade, when a kid with a sleepy eye and two streams of mucus depending from his nostrils hit me in the knee with a Louisville slugger; never mind that I'd touched the tire iron exactly twice before, to change tires: it was there. And I went for it.

I was terrified. Blood was beating in my ears, my hands were shaking, my heart turning over like a dirtbike in the wrong gear. My antagonist was shirtless, and a single cord of muscle flashed across his chest as he bent forward to peel Jeff from his back like a wet overcoat. "Motherfucker," he spat, over and over, and I was aware in that instant that all four of us—Digby, Jeff, and myself included—were chanting "motherfucker, motherfucker," as if it were a battle cry. (What happened next? the detective asks the murderer from beneath the turned-down brim of his porkpie hat. I don't know, the murderer says, something came over me. Exactly.)

Digby poked the flat of his hand in the bad character's face and I came at him like a kamikaze, mindless, raging, stung with humiliation—the whole thing, from the initial boot in the chin to this murderous primal instant involving no more than sixty hyperventilating, gland-flooding seconds—and I came at him and brought the tire iron down across his ear. The effect was instantaneous, astonishing. He was a stuntman and this was Hollywood, he was a big grimacing toothy balloon and I was a man with a straight pin. He collapsed. Wet his pants. Went loose in his boots.

A single second, big as a zeppelin, floated by. We were standing over him in a circle, gritting our teeth, jerking our necks, our limbs and hands and feet twitching with glandular discharges. No one said anything. We just stared down at the guy, the car freak, the lover, the bad greasy character laid low. Digby looked at me; so did Jeff. I was still holding the tire iron, a tuft of hair clinging to the crook like dandelion fluff, like down. Rattled, I dropped it in the dirt, already envisioning the headlines, the pitted faces of the police inquisitors, the gleam of handcuffs, clank of bars, the big black shadows rising from the back of the cell . . . when suddenly a raw torn shriek cut through me like all the juice in all the electric chairs in the country.

It was the fox. She was short, barefoot, dressed in panties and a man's shirt. "Animals!" she screamed, running at us with her fists clenched and wisps of blow-dried hair in her face. There was a silver chain round her ankle, and her toenails flashed in the glare of the headlights. I think it was the toenails that did it. Sure, the gin and the cannabis and even the Kentucky Fried may have had a hand in it, but it was the sight of those flaming toes that set us off—the toad emerging from the loaf in *Virgin Spring*, lipstick smeared on a child: she was already tainted. We were on her like Bergman's deranged brothers—see no evil, hear none, speak none—panting, wheezing, tearing at her clothes, grabbing for flesh. We were bad characters, and we were scared and hot and three steps over the line—anything could have happened.

It didn't.

Before we could pin her to the hood of the car, our eyes masked with lust and greed and the purest primal badness, a pair of headlights swung into the lot. There we were, dirty, bloody, guilty, dissociated from humanity and civilization, the first of the Ur-crimes behind us, the second in progress, shreds of nylon panty and spandex brassiere dangling from our fingers, our flies open, lips licked—there we were, caught in the spotlight. Nailed.

We bolted. First for the car, and then, realizing we had no way of starting it, for the woods. I thought nothing. I thought escape. The headlights came at me like accusing fingers. I was gone.

Ram-bam-bam, across the parking lot, past the chopper and into the feculent undergrowth at the lake's edge, insects flying up in my face, weeds whipping, frogs and snakes and red-eyed turtles splashing off into the night: I was already ankle-deep in muck and tepid water and still going strong. Behind me, the girl's screams rose in intensity, disconsolate, incriminating, the screams of the Sabine women, the Christian martyrs, Anne Frank dragged from the garret. I kept going, pursued by those cries, imagining cops and bloodhounds. The water was up to my knees when I realized what I was doing: I was going to swim for it. Swim the breadth of Greasy Lake and hide myself in the thick clot of woods on the far side. They'd never find me there.

I was breathing in sobs, in gasps. The water lapped at my waist as I looked out over the moon-burnished ripples, the mats of algae that clung to the surface like scabs. Digby and Jeff had vanished. I paused. Listened. The girl was quieter now, screams tapering to sobs, but there were male voices, angry, excited, and the high-pitched ticking of the second car's engine. I waded deeper, stealthy, hunted, the ooze sucking at my sneakers. As I was about to take the plunge—at the very instant I dropped my shoulder for the first slashing stroke—I blundered into something. Something unspeakable, obscene, something soft, wet, moss-grown. A patch of weed? A log? When I reached out to touch it, it gave like a rubber duck, it gave like flesh.

In one of those nasty little epiphanies for which we are prepared by films and TV and childhood visits to the funeral home to ponder the shrunken painted forms of dead grandparents, I understood what it was that bobbed there so inadmissibly in the dark. Understood, and stumbled back in horror and revulsion, my mind yanked in six different directions (I was nineteen, a mere child, an infant, and here in the space of five minutes I'd struck down one greasy character and blundered into the waterlogged carcass of a second), thinking, The keys, the keys, why did I have to go and lose the keys? I stumbled back, but the muck took hold of my feet—a sneaker snagged, balance lost—and suddenly I was pitching face forward into the buoyant black mass, throwing out my hands in desperation while simultaneously conjuring the image of reeking frogs and muskrats revolving in slicks of their own deliquescing juices. AAAAArrrgh! I shot from the water like a torpedo, the dead man rotating to expose a mossy beard and eyes cold as the moon. I must have shouted out, thrashing around in the weeds, because the voices behind me suddenly became animated.

"What was that?"

"It's them, it's them: they tried to, tried to . . . *rape* me!" Sobs.

A man's voice, flat, Midwestern accent. "You sons a bitches, we'll kill you!"

Frogs, crickets.

Then another voice, harsh, *r*-less, Lower East Side: "Motherfucker!" I recognized the verbal virtuosity of the bad greasy character in the engineer boots. Tooth chipped, sneakers gone, coated in mud and slime and worse, crouching breathless in the weeds waiting to have my ass thoroughly and definitively kicked and fresh from the hideous stinking embrace of a three-days-dead corpse, I suddenly felt a rush of joy and vindication: the son of a bitch was alive! Just as quickly, my bowels turned to ice. "Come on out of there, you pansy motherfuckers!" the bad greasy character was screaming. He shouted curses till he was out of breath.

The crickets started up again, then the frogs. I held my breath. All at once there was a sound in the reeds, a swishing, a splash: thunk-a-thunk. They were throwing rocks. The frogs fell silent. I cradled my head. Swish, swish, thunk-a-thunk. A wedge of feldspar the size of a cue ball glanced off my knee. I bit my finger.

It was then that they turned to the car. I heard a door slam, a curse, and then the sound of the headlights shattering—almost a good-natured sound, celebratory, like corks popping from the necks of bottles. This was succeeded by the dull booming of the fenders, metal on metal, and then the icy crash of the windshield. I inched forward, elbows and knees, my belly pressed to the muck, thinking of guerrillas and commandos and *The Naked and the Dead*. I parted the weeds and squinted the length of the parking lot.

The second car—it was a Trans-Am—was still running, its high beams washing the scene in a lurid stagy light. Tire iron flailing, the greasy bad character was laying into the side of my mother's Bel Air like an avenging demon, his shadow riding up the trunks of the trees. Whomp. Whomp. Whomp-whomp. The other two guys—blond types, in fraternity jackets—were helping out with tree branches and skull-sized boulders. One of them was gathering up bottles, rocks, muck, candy wrappers, used condoms, poptops, and other refuse and pitching it through the window on the driver's side. I could see the fox, a white bulb behind the windshield of the '57 Chevy. "Bobbie," she whined over the thumping, "come *on*." The greasy character paused a moment, took one good swipe at the left taillight, and then heaved the tire iron halfway across the lake. Then he fired up the '57 and was gone.

Blond head nodded at blond head. One said something to the other, too low for me to catch. They were no doubt thinking that in helping to annihilate my mother's car they'd committed a fairly rash act, and thinking too that there were three bad characters connected with that very car watching them from the woods. Perhaps other possibilities occurred to them as well—police, jail cells, justices of the peace, reparations, lawyers, irate parents, fraternal censure. Whatever they were thinking, they suddenly dropped branches, bottles, and rocks and sprang for their car in unison, as if they'd choreographed it. Five seconds. That's all it took. The engine shrieked, the tires squealed, a cloud of dust rose from the rutted lot and then settled back on darkness.

I don't know how long I lay there, the bad breath of decay all around me, my jacket heavy as a bear, the primordial ooze subtly reconstituting itself to accommodate my upper thighs and testicles. My jaws ached, my knee throbbed, my coccyx was on fire. I contemplated suicide, wondered if I'd need bridgework, scraped the recesses of my brain for some sort of excuse to give my parents—a tree had fallen on the car, I was blindsided by a bread truck, hit and run, vandals had got to it while we were playing chess at Digby's. Then I thought of the dead man. He was probably the only person on the planet worse off than I was: I thought about him, fog on the lake, insects chirring eerily, and felt the tug of fear, felt the darkness opening up inside me like a set of jaws. Who was he? I wondered, this victim of time and circumstance bobbing sorrowfully in the lake at my back. The owner of the chopper, no doubt, a bad older character come to this. Shot during a murky drug deal, drowned while drunkenly frolicking in the lake. Another headline. My car was wrecked; he was dead.

When the eastern half of the sky went from black to cobalt and the trees began to separate themselves from the shadows, I pushed myself up from the mud and stepped out into the open. By now the birds had begun to take over for the crickets, and dew lay slick on the leaves. There was a smell in the air, raw and sweet at the same time, the smell of the sun firing buds and opening blossoms. I contemplated the car. It lay there like a wreck along the highway, like a steel sculpture left over from a vanished civilization. Everything was still. This was nature.

I was circling the car, as dazed and bedraggled as the sole survivor of an air blitz, when Digby and Jeff emerged from the trees behind me. Digby's face was crosshatched with smears of dirt; Jeff's jacket was gone and his shirt was torn across the shoulder. They slouched across the lot, looking sheepish, and silently came up beside me to gape at the ravaged automobile. No one said a word. After a while Jeff swung open the driver's door and began to scoop the broken glass and garbage off the seat. I looked at Digby. He shrugged. "At least they didn't slash the tires," he said.

It was true: the tires were intact. There was no windshield, the headlights were staved in, and the body looked as if it had been sledgehammered for a quarter a shot at the county fair, but the tires were inflated to regulation pressure. The car was drivable. In silence, all three of us bent to scrape the mud and shattered glass from the interior. I said nothing about the biker. When we were finished, I reached in my pocket for the keys, experienced a nasty stab of recollection, cursed myself, and turned to search the grass. I spotted them almost immediately, no more than five feet from the open door, glinting like jewels in the first tapering shaft of sunlight. There was no reason to get philosophical about it: I eased into the seat and turned the engine over.

It was at that precise moment that the silver Mustang with the flame decals rumbled into the lot. All three of us froze; then Digby and Jeff slid into the car and slammed the door. We watched as the Mustang rocked and bobbed across the ruts and finally jerked to a halt beside the forlorn chopper at the far end of the lot.

"Let's go," Digby said. I hesitated, the Bel Air wheezing beneath me.

Two girls emerged from the Mustang. Tight jeans, stiletto heels, hair like frozen fur. They bent over the motorcycle, paced back and forth aimlessly, glanced once or twice at us, and then ambled over to where the reeds sprang up in a green fence round the perimeter of the lake. One of them cupped her hands to her mouth. "Al," she called. "Hey, Al!"

"Come on," Digby hissed. "Let's get out of here."

But it was too late. The second girl was picking her way across the lot, unsteady on her heels, looking up at us and then away. She was older—twenty-five or -six—and as she came closer we could see there was something wrong with her: she was stoned or drunk, lurching now and waving her arms for balance. I gripped the steering wheel as if it were the ejection lever of a flaming jet, and Digby spat out my name, twice, terse and impatient.

"Hi," the girl said.

We looked at her like zombies, like war veterans, like deaf-and-dumb pencil peddlers.

She smiled, her lips cracked and dry. "Listen," she said, bending from the waist to look in the window, "you guys seen Al?" Her pupils were pinpoints, her eyes glass. She jerked her neck. "That's his bike over there—Al's. You seen him?"

Al. I didn't know what to say. I wanted to get out of the car and retch, I wanted to go home to my parents' house and crawl into bed. Digby poked me in the ribs. "We haven't seen anybody," I said.

The girl seemed to consider this, reaching out a slim veiny arm to brace herself against the car. "No matter," she said, slurring the *t*'s, "he'll turn up." And then, as if she'd just taken stock of the whole scene—the ravaged car and our battered faces, the desolation of the place—she said: "Hey, you guys look like some pretty bad characters—been fightin', huh?" We stared straight ahead, rigid as catatonics. She was fumbling in her pocket and muttering something. Finally she held out a handful of tablets in glassine wrappers: "Hey, you want to party, you want to do some of these with me and Sarah?"

I just looked at her. I thought I was going to cry. Digby broke the silence. "No thanks," he said, leaning over me. "Some other time."

I put the car in gear and it inched forward with a groan, shaking off pellets of glass like an old dog shedding water after a bath, heaving over the ruts on its worn springs, creeping toward the highway. There was a sheen of sun on the lake. I looked back. The girl was still standing there, watching us, her shoulders slumped, hand outstretched.

(1981)

THE LOVE OF MY LIFE

They wore each other like a pair of socks. He was at her house, she was at his. Everywhere they went—to the mall, to the game, to movies and shops and the classes that structured their days like a new kind of chronology—their fingers were entwined, their shoulders touching, their hips joined in the slow triumphant sashay of love. He drove her car, slept on the couch in the family room at her parents' house, played tennis and watched football with her father on the big thirty-six-inch TV in the kitchen. She went shopping with his mother and hers, a triumvirate of tastes, and she would have played tennis with his father, if it came to it, but his father was dead. "I love you," he told her, because he did, because there was no feeling like this, no triumph, no high—it was like being immortal and unconquerable, like floating. And a hundred times a day she said it too: "I love you. I love you."

They were together at his house one night when the rain froze on the streets and sheathed the trees in glass. It was her idea to take a walk and feel it in their hair and on the glistening shoulders of their parkas, an otherworldly drumming of pellets flung down out of the troposphere, alien and familiar at the same time, and they glided the length of the front walk and watched the way the power lines bellied and swayed. He built a fire when they got back, while she toweled her hair and made hot chocolate laced with Jack Daniel's. They'd rented a pair of slasher movies for the ritualized comfort of them—"Teens have sex," he said, "and then they pay for it in body parts"—and the maniac had just climbed out of the heating vent, with a meat hook dangling from the recesses of his empty sleeve, when the phone rang.

It was his mother, calling from the hotel room in Boston where she was curled up—shacked up?—for the weekend with the man she'd been dating. He tried to picture her, but he couldn't. He even closed his eyes a minute, to concentrate, but there was nothing there. Was everything all right? she wanted to know. With the storm and all? No, it hadn't hit Boston yet, but she saw on the Weather Channel that it was on its way. Two seconds after he hung up—before she could even hit the Start button on the VCR—the phone rang again, and this time it was her mother. Her mother had been drinking. She was calling from a restaurant, and China could hear a clamor of voices in the background. "Just stay put," her mother shouted into the phone. "The streets are like a skating rink. Don't you even think of getting in that car."

Well, she wasn't thinking of it. She was thinking of having Jeremy to herself, all night, in the big bed in his mother's room. They'd been having sex ever since they started going together at the end of their junior year, but it was always sex in the car or sex on a blanket or the lawn, hurried sex, nothing like she wanted it to be. She kept thinking of the way it was in the movies, where the stars ambushed each other on beds the size of small planets and then did it again and again until they lay nestled in a heap of pillows and blankets, her head on his chest, his arm flung over her shoulder, the music fading away to individual notes plucked softly on a guitar and everything in the frame glowing as if it had been sprayed with liquid gold. That was how it was supposed to be. That was how it was going to be. At least for tonight.

She'd been wandering around the kitchen as she talked, dancing with the phone in an idle slow saraband, watching the frost sketch a design on the window over the sink, no sound but the soft hiss of the ice pellets on the roof, and now she pulled open the freezer door and extracted a pint box of ice cream. She was in her socks, socks so thick they were like slippers, and a pair of black leggings under an over-sized sweater. Beneath her feet, the polished floorboards were as slick as the sidewalk outside, and she liked the feel of that, skating indoors in her big socks. "Uh-huh," she said into the phone. "Uh-huh. Yeah, we're watching a movie." She dug a finger into the ice cream and stuck it in her mouth.

"Come on," Jeremy called from the living room, where the maniac rippled menacingly over the Pause button. "You're going to miss the best part."

"Okay, Mom, okay," she said into the phone, parting words, and then she hung up. "You want ice cream?" she called, licking her finger.

Jeremy's voice came back at her, a voice in the middle range, with a congenital scratch in it, the voice of a nice guy, a very nice guy who could be the star of a TV show about nice guys: "What kind?" He had a pair of shoulders and pumped-up biceps too, a smile that jumped from his lips to his eyes, and close-cropped hair that stood up straight off the crown of his head. And he was always singing—she loved that—his voice so true he could do any song, and there was no lyric he didn't know, even on the oldies station. She scooped ice cream and saw him in a scene from last summer, one hand draped casually over the wheel of his car, the radio throbbing, his voice raised in perfect sync with Billy Corgan's, and the night standing still at the end of a long dark street overhung with maples.

"Chocolate. Swiss chocolate almond."

"Okay," he said, and then he was wondering if there was any whipped cream, or maybe hot fudge—he was sure his mother had a jar stashed away somewhere, *Look behind the mayonnaise on the top row*—and when she turned around he was standing in the doorway.

She kissed him—they kissed whenever they met, no matter where or when, even if one of them had just stepped out of the room, because that was love, that was the way love was—and then they took two bowls of ice cream into the living room and, with a flick of the remote, set the maniac back in motion.

It was an early spring that year, the world gone green overnight, the thermometer twice hitting the low eighties in the first week of March. Teachers were holding sessions outside. The whole school, even the halls and the cafeteria, smelled of fresh-mowed grass and the unfolding blossoms of the fruit trees in the development across the street, and students—especially seniors—were cutting class to go out to the quarry or the reservoir or to just drive the back streets with the sunroof and the windows open wide. But not China. She was hitting the books, studying late, putting everything in its place like pegs in a board, even love, even that. Jeremy didn't get it. "Look, you've already been accepted at your first-choice school, you're going to wind up in the top ten G.P.A.-wise, and you've got four years of tests and term papers ahead of you, and grad school after that. You'll only be a high-school senior once in your life. Relax. Enjoy it. Or at least *experience* it."

He'd been accepted at Brown, his father's alma mater, and his own G.P.A. would put him in the top ten percent of their graduating class, and he was content with that, skating through his final semester, no math, no science, taking art and music, the things he'd always wanted to take but never had time for—and Lit, of course, A.P. History, and Spanish 5. "*Tú eres el amor de mi vida*," he would tell her when they met at her locker or at lunch or when he picked her up for a movie on Saturday nights.

"*Y tú también*," she would say, "or is it '*yo también*'?"—French was her language. "But I keep telling you it really matters to me, because I know I'll never catch Margery Yu or Christian Davenport, I mean they're a lock for val and salut, but it'll kill me if people like

King, and then it was the sun and the wind and the moon and the stars. Five days. Five whole days.

"Yeah," he said, in answer to her question, "my mother said she didn't want to have to worry about us breaking down in the middle of nowhere—"

"So she's got your car? She's going to sell real estate in your car?"

He just shrugged and smiled. "Free at last," he said, pitching his voice down low till it was exactly like Martin Luther King's. "Thank God Almighty, we are free at last."

It was dark by the time they got to the trailhead, and they wound up camping just off the road in a rocky tumble of brush, no place on earth less likely or less comfortable, but they were together, and they held each other through the damp whispering hours of the night and hardly slept at all. They made the lake by noon the next day, the trees just coming into leaf, the air sweet with the smell of the sun in the pines. She insisted on setting up the tent, just in case—it could rain, you never knew—but all he wanted to do was stretch out on a gray neoprene pad and feel the sun on his face. Eventually, they both fell asleep in the sun, and when they woke they made love right there, beneath the trees, and with the wide blue expanse of the lake giving back the blue of the sky. For dinner, it was étouffée and rice, out of the foil pouch, washed down with hot chocolate and a few squirts of red wine from Jeremy's bota bag.

The next day, the whole day through, they didn't bother with clothes at all. They couldn't swim, of course—the lake was too cold for that—but they could bask and explore and feel the breeze out of the south on their bare legs and the places where no breeze had touched before. She would remember that always, the feel of that, the intensity of her emotions, the simple unrefined pleasure of living in the moment. Woodsmoke. Dueling flashlights in the night. The look on Jeremy's face when he presented her with the bag of finger-sized crayfish he'd spent all morning collecting.

What else? The rain, of course. It came midway through the

Kerry Sharp or Jalapy Seegrand finish ahead of me—
know that, you of all people—"

It amazed him that she actually brought her books
they went backpacking over spring break. They'd p
trip all winter and through the long wind tunnel that wa
packing away freeze-dried entrées, Power Bars, Gore-
breakers and matching sweatshirts, weighing each item
held scale with a dangling hook at the bottom of it. They
up into the Catskills, to a lake he'd found on a map, and
going to be together, without interruption, without
automobiles, parents, teachers, friends, relatives, and pe
full days. They were going to cook over an open fire,
going to read to each other and burrow into the double sl
with the connubial zipper up the seam he'd found in hi
closet, a relic of her own time in the lap of nature. It smel
of his mother, a vague scent of her perfume that had ling
dormant all these years, and maybe there was the faintest v
father too, though his father had been gone so long he
remember what he looked like, let alone what he might ha
like. Five days. And it wasn't going to rain, not a drop.
even bring his fishing rod, and that was love.

When the last bell rang down the curtain on Hon
Jeremy was waiting at the curb in his mother's Volvo stati
grinning up at China through the windshield while the
school swept past with no thought for anything but relea
were shouts and curses, T-shirts in motion, slashing le
bleating from the seniors' lot, the school buses lined up like
vehicles awaiting the invasion—chaos, sweet chaos—and
there a moment to savor it. "Your mother's car?" she said
in beside him and laying both arms over his shoulders to pi
her for a kiss. He'd brought her jeans and hiking boots a
she was going to change as they drove, no need to go home,
circumvention and delay, a stop at McDonald's, maybe,

third day, clouds the color of iron filings, the lake hammered to iron too, and the storm that crashed through the trees and beat at their tent with a thousand angry fists. They huddled in the sleeping bag, sharing the wine and a bag of trail mix, reading to each other from a book of Donne's love poems (she was writing a paper for Mrs. Masterson called "Ocular Imagery in the Poetry of John Donne") and the last third of a vampire novel that weighed eighteen-point-one ounces.

And the sex. They were careful, always careful—*I will never, never be like those breeders that bring their puffed-up squalling little red-faced babies to class*, she told him, and he agreed, got adamant about it, even, until it became a running theme in their relationship, the breeders overpopulating an overpopulated world and ruining their own lives in the process—but she had forgotten to pack her pills and he had only two condoms with him, and it wasn't as if there was a drugstore around the corner.

In the fall—or the end of August, actually—they packed their cars separately and left for college, he to Providence and she to Binghamton. They were separated by three hundred miles, but there was the telephone, there was e-mail, and for the first month or so there were Saturday nights in a motel in Danbury, but that was a haul, it really was, and they both agreed that they should focus on their course work and cut back to every second or maybe third week. On the day they'd left—and no, she didn't want her parents driving her up there, she was an adult and she could take care of herself—Jeremy followed her as far as the Bear Mountain Bridge and they pulled off the road and held each other till the sun fell down into the trees. She had a poem for him, a Donne poem, the saddest thing he'd ever heard. It was something about the moon. *More than moon*, that was it, lovers parting and their tears swelling like an ocean till the girl—the woman, the female—had more power to raise the tides than the moon itself, or some such. More than moon. That's what he called her after that, because she was white and round and getting rounder, and it was no joke, and it was no term of endearment.

She was pregnant. Pregnant, they figured, since the camping trip, and it was their secret, a new constant in their lives, a fact, an inescapable fact that never varied no matter how many home pregnancy kits they went through. Baggy clothes, that was the key, all in black, cargo pants, flowing dresses, a jacket even in summer. They went to a store in the city where nobody knew them and she got a girdle, and then she went away to school in Binghamton and he went to Providence. "You've got to get rid of it," he told her in the motel room that had become a prison. "Go to a clinic," he told her for the hundredth time, and outside it was raining—or, no, it was clear and cold that night, a foretaste of winter. "I'll find the money—you know I will."

She wouldn't respond. Wouldn't even look at him. One of the *Star Wars* movies was on TV, great flat thundering planes of metal roaring across the screen, and she was just sitting there on the edge of the bed, her shoulders hunched and hair hanging limp. Someone slammed a car door—two doors in rapid succession—and a child's voice shouted, "Me! Me first!"

"China," he said. "Are you listening to me?"

"I can't," she murmured, and she was talking to her lap, to the bed, to the floor. "I'm scared. I'm so scared." There were footsteps in the room next door, ponderous and heavy, then the quick tattoo of the child's feet and a sudden thump against the wall. "I don't want anyone to know," she said.

He could have held her, could have squeezed in beside her and wrapped her in his arms, but something flared in him. He couldn't understand it. He just couldn't. "What are you thinking? Nobody'll know. He's a doctor, for Christ's sake, sworn to secrecy, the doctor-patient compact and all that. What are you going to do, keep it? Huh? Just show up for English 101 with a baby on your lap and say, 'Hi, I'm the Virgin Mary'?"

She was crying. He could see it in the way her shoulders suddenly crumpled and now he could hear it too, a soft nasal complaint that went right through him. She lifted her face to him and held out her arms and he was there beside her, rocking her back and forth in his arms. He could feel the heat of her face against the hard fiber of his chest, a wetness there, fluids, her fluids. "I don't want a doctor," she said.

And that colored everything, that simple negative: life in the dorms, roommates, bars, bullshit sessions, the smell of burning leaves and the way the light fell across campus in great wide smoking bands just before dinner, the unofficial skateboard club, films, lectures, pep rallies, football—none of it mattered. He couldn't have a life. Couldn't be a freshman. Couldn't wake up in the morning and tumble into the slow steady current of the world. All he could think of was her. Or not simply her—her and him, and what had come between them. Because they argued now, they wrangled and fought and debated, and it was no pleasure to see her in that motel room with the queen-size bed and the big color TV and the soaps and shampoos they made off with as if they were treasure. She was pigheaded, stubborn, irrational. She was spoiled, he could see that now, spoiled by her parents and their standard of living and the socioeconomic expectations of her class—of his class—and the promise of life as you like it, an unscrolling vista of pleasure and acquisition. He loved her. He didn't want to turn his back on her. He would be there for her no matter what, but why did she have to be so *stupid*?

Big sweats, huge sweats, sweats that drowned and engulfed her, that was her campus life, sweats and the dining hall. Her dormmates didn't know her, and so what if she was putting on weight? Everybody did. How could you shovel down all those carbohydrates, all that sugar and grease and the puddings and nachos and all the rest, without putting on ten or fifteen pounds the first semester alone? Half the girls in the dorm were waddling around like the Doughboy, their faces bloated and blotched with acne, with crusting pimples and whiteheads fed on fat. So she was putting on weight. Big deal. "There's more of me to love," she told her roommate, "and Jeremy likes it that way. And, really, he's the only one that matters." She was careful to shower alone, in the early morning, long before the light had begun to bump up against the windows.

On the night her water broke—it was mid-December, almost nine months, as best as she could figure—it was raining. Raining hard. All week she'd been having tense rasping sotto voce debates with Jeremy on the phone—arguments, fights—and she told him that she would die, creep out into the woods like some animal and bleed to death, before she'd go to a hospital. "And what am I supposed to do?" he demanded in a high childish whine, as if he were the one who'd been knocked up, and she didn't want to hear it, she didn't.

"Do you love me?" she whispered. There was a long hesitation, a pause you could have poured all the affirmation of the world into.

"Yes," he said finally, his voice so soft and reluctant it was like the last gasp of a dying old man.

"Then you're going to have to rent the motel."

"And then what?"

"Then—I don't know." The door was open, her roommate framed there in the hall, a burst of rock and roll coming at her like an assault. "I guess you'll have to get a book or something."

By eight, the rain had turned to ice and every branch of every tree was coated with it, the highway littered with glistening black sticks, no moon, no stars, the tires sliding out from under her, and she felt heavy, big as a sumo wrestler, heavy and loose at the same time. She'd taken a towel from the dorm and put it under her, on the seat, but it was a mess, everything was a mess. She was cramping. Fidgeting with her hair. She tried the radio, but it was no help, nothing but songs she hated, singers that were worse. Twenty-two miles to Danbury, and the first of the contractions came like a seizure, like a knife blade thrust into her spine. Her world narrowed to what the headlights would show her.

Jeremy was waiting for her at the door to the room, the light behind him a pale rinse of nothing, no smile on his face, no human expression at all. They didn't kiss—they didn't even touch—and then she was on the bed, on her back, her face clenched like a fist. She heard the rattle of the sleet at the window, the murmur of the TV: *I can't let you go like this*, a man protested, and she could picture him, angular and tall, a man in a hat and overcoat in a black-and-white world that might have been another planet, *I just can't*. "Are you—?" Jeremy's voice drifted into the mix, and then stalled. "Are you ready? I mean, is it time? Is it coming now?"

She said one thing then, one thing only, her voice as pinched and hollow as the sound of the wind in the gutters: "Get it out of me."

It took a moment, and then she could feel his hands fumbling with her sweats.

Later, hours later, when nothing had happened but pain, a parade of pain with drum majors and brass bands and penitents crawling on their hands and knees till the streets were stained with their blood, she cried out and cried out again. "It's like *Alien*," she gasped, "like that thing in *Alien* when it, it—"

"It's okay," he kept telling her, "it's okay," but his face betrayed him. He looked scared, looked as if he'd been drained of blood in some evil experiment in yet another movie, and a part of her wanted to be sorry for him, but another part, the part that was so commanding and fierce it overrode everything else, couldn't begin to be.

He was useless, and he knew it. He'd never been so purely sick at heart and terrified in all his life, but he tried to be there for her, tried to do his best, and when the baby came out, the baby girl all slick with blood and mucus and the lumped white stuff that was like something spilled at the bottom of a garbage can, he was thinking of the ninth grade and how close he'd come to fainting while the teacher went around the room to prick their fingers one by one so they each could smear a drop of blood across a slide. He didn't faint now. But he was close to it, so close he could feel the room dodging away under his feet. And then her voice, the first intelligible thing she'd said in an hour: "Get rid of it. Just get rid of it."

Of the drive back to Binghamton he remembered nothing. Or practically nothing. They took towels from the motel and spread them across the seat of her car, he could remember that much . . . and the blood, how could he forget the blood? It soaked through her sweats and the towels and even the thick cotton bathmat and into the worn fabric of the seat itself. And it all came from inside her, all of it, tissue and mucus and the shining bright fluid, no end to it, as if she'd been turned inside out. He wanted to ask her about that, if that was normal, but she was asleep the minute she slid out from under his arm and dropped into the seat. If he focused, if he really concentrated, he could remember the way her head lolled against the doorframe while the engine whined and the car rocked and the slush threw a dark blanket over the windshield every time a truck shot past in the opposite direction. That and the exhaustion. He'd never been so tired, his head on a string, shoulders slumped, his arms like two pillars of concrete. And what if he'd nodded off? What if he'd gone into a skid and hurtled over an embankment into the filthy gray accumulation of the worst day of his life? What then?

She made it into the dorm under her own power, nobody even looked at her, and no, she didn't need his help. "Call me," she whispered, and they kissed, her lips so cold it was like kissing a steak through the plastic wrapper, and then he parked her car in the student lot and walked to the bus station. He made Danbury late that night, caught a ride out to the motel, and walked right through the Do Not Disturb sign on the door. Fifteen minutes. That was all it took. He bundled up everything, every trace, left the key in the box at the desk, and stood scraping the ice off the windshield of his car while the night opened up above him to a black glitter of sky. He never gave a thought to what lay discarded in the Dumpster out back, itself wrapped in plastic, so much meat, so much cold meat.

■ ■ ■

He was at the very pinnacle of his dream, the river dressed in its currents, the deep hole under the cutbank, and the fish like silver bullets
swarming to his bait, when they woke him—when Rob woke him,
Rob Greiner, his roommate, Rob with a face of crumbling stone and
two policemen there at the door behind him and the roar of the
dorm falling away to a whisper. And that was strange, policemen, a
real anomaly in that setting, and at first—for the first thirty seconds,
at least—he had no idea what they were doing there. Parking tickets?
Could that be it? But then they asked him his name, just to confirm
it, joined his hands together behind his back, and fitted two loops of
naked metal over his wrists, and he began to understand. He saw
McCaffrey and Tuttle from across the hall staring at him as if he
were Jeffrey Dahmer or something, and the rest of them, all the rest,
every head poking out of every door up and down the corridor, as
the police led him away.

"What's this all about?" he kept saying, the cruiser nosing
through the dark streets to the station house, the man at the wheel
and the man beside him as incapable of speech as the seats or the wire
mesh or the gleaming black dashboard that dragged them forward
into the night. And then it was up the steps and into an explosion of
light, more men in uniform, stand here, give me your hand, now the
other one, and then the cage and the questions. Only then did he
think of that thing in the garbage sack and the sound it had made—
its body had made—when he flung it into the Dumpster like a sack
of flour and the lid slammed down on it. He stared at the walls, and
this was a movie too. He'd never been in trouble before, never been
inside a police station, but he knew his role well enough, because he'd
seen it played out a thousand times on the tube: deny everything.
Even as the two detectives settled in across from him at the bare
wooden table in the little box of the overlit room he was telling
himself just that: *Deny it, deny it all.*

The first detective leaned forward and set his hands on the table as if he'd come for a manicure. He was in his thirties, or maybe his forties, a tired-looking man with the scars of the turmoil he'd witnessed gouged into the flesh under his eyes. He didn't offer a cigarette ("I don't smoke," Jeremy was prepared to say, giving them that much at least), and he didn't smile or soften his eyes. And when he spoke his voice carried no freight at all, not outrage or threat or cajolery—it was just a voice, flat and tired. "Do you know a China Berkowitz?" he said.

And she. She was in the community hospital, where the ambulance had deposited her after her roommate had called 911 in a voice that was like a bone stuck in the back of her throat, and it was raining again. Her parents were there, her mother red-eyed and sniffling, her father looking like an actor who's forgotten his lines, and there was another woman there too, a policewoman. The policewoman sat in an orange plastic chair in the corner, dipping her head to the knitting in her lap. At first, China's mother had tried to be pleasant to the woman, but pleasant wasn't what the circumstances called for, and now she ignored her, because the very unpleasant fact was that China was being taken into custody as soon as she was released from the hospital.

For a long while no one said anything—everything had already been said, over and over, one long flood of hurt and recrimination—and the antiseptic silence of the hospital held them in its grip while the rain beat at the windows and the machines at the foot of the bed counted off numbers. From down the hall came a snatch of TV dialogue, and for a minute China opened her eyes and thought she was back in the dorm. "Honey," her mother said, raising a purgatorial face to her, "are you all right? Can I get you anything?"

"I need to—I think I need to pee."

"Why?" her father demanded, and it was the perfect non sequitur. He was up out of the chair, standing over her, his eyes like cracked porcelain. "Why didn't you tell us, or at least tell your mother—or Dr. Fredman? Dr. Fredman, at least. He's been—he's like a family member, you know that, and he could have, or he would have . . . What were you *thinking*, for Christ's sake?"

Thinking? She wasn't thinking anything, not then and not now. All she wanted—and she didn't care what they did to her, beat her, torture her, drag her weeping through the streets in a dirty white dress with "Baby Killer" stitched over her breast in scarlet letters— was to see Jeremy. Just that. Because what really mattered was what he was thinking.

The food at the Sarah Barnes Cooper Women's Correctional Institute was exactly what they served at the dining hall in college, heavy on the sugars, starches, and bad cholesterol, and that would have struck her as ironic if she'd been there under other circumstances—doing community outreach, say, or researching a paper for her sociology class. But given the fact that she'd been locked up for more than a month now, the object of the other girls' threats, scorn, and just plain *nastiness*, given the fact that her life was ruined beyond any hope of redemption, and every newspaper in the country had her shrunken white face plastered across its front page under a headline that screamed MOTEL MOM, she didn't have much use for irony. She was scared twenty-four hours a day. Scared of the present, scared of the future, scared of the reporters waiting for the judge to set bail so that they could swarm all over her the minute she stepped out the door. She couldn't concentrate on the books and magazines her mother brought her or even on the TV in the rec room. She sat in her room—it was a room, just like a dorm room, except that they locked you in at night—and stared at the walls, eating peanuts, M&M's, sunflower seeds by the handful, chewing for the pure animal gratification of it. She was putting on more weight, and what did it matter?

Jeremy was different. He'd lost everything—his walk, his smile, the muscles of his upper arms and shoulders. Even his hair lay flat now, as if he couldn't bother with a tube of gel and a comb. When she saw him at the arraignment, saw him for the first time since she'd climbed out of the car and limped into the dorm with the blood wet on her legs, he looked like a refugee, like a ghost. The room they were in—the courtroom—seemed to have grown up around them, walls, windows, benches, lights, and radiators already in place, along with the judge, the American flag, and the ready-made spectators. It was hot. People coughed into their fists and shuffled their feet, every sound magnified. The judge presided, his arms like bones twirled in a bag, his eyes searching and opaque as he peered over the top of his reading glasses.

China's lawyer didn't like Jeremy's lawyer, that much was evident, and the state prosecutor didn't like anybody. She watched him—Jeremy, only him—as the reporters held their collective breath and the judge read off the charges and her mother bowed her head and sobbed into the bucket of her hands. And Jeremy was watching her too, his eyes locked on hers as if he defied them all, as if nothing mattered in the world but her, and when the judge said "First-degree murder" and "Murder by abuse or neglect," he never flinched.

She sent him a note that day—"I love you, will always love you no matter what, More than Moon"—and in the hallway, afterward, while their lawyers fended off the reporters and the bailiffs tugged impatiently at them, they had a minute, just a minute, to themselves. "What did you tell them?" he whispered. His voice was a rasp, almost a growl; she looked at him, inches away, and hardly recognized him.

"I told them it was dead."

"My lawyer—Mrs. Teagues?—she says they're saying it was alive when we, when we put it in the bag." His face was composed, but his eyes were darting like insects trapped inside his head.

"It was dead."

"It looked dead," he said, and already he was pulling away from her and some callous shit with a camera kept annihilating them with flash after flash of light, "and we certainly didn't—I mean, we didn't slap it or anything to get it breathing. . . ."

And then the last thing he said to her, just as they were pulled apart, and it was nothing she wanted to hear, nothing that had any love in it, or even the hint of love: "You told me to get rid of it."

There was no elaborate name for the place where they were keeping him. It was known as Drum Hill Prison, period. No reform-minded notions here, no verbal gestures toward rehabilitation or behavior modification, no benefactors, mayors, or role models to lend the place their family names, but then who in his right mind would want a prison named after him anyway? At least they kept him separated from the other prisoners, the gangbangers and dope dealers and sexual predators and the like. He was no longer a freshman at Brown, not officially, but he had his books and his course notes, and he tried to keep up as best he could. Still, when the screams echoed through the cellblock at night and the walls dripped with the accumulated breath of eight and a half thousand terminally angry sociopaths, he had to admit it wasn't the sort of college experience he'd bargained for.

And what had he done to deserve it? He still couldn't understand. That thing in the Dumpster—and he refused to call it human, let alone a baby—was nobody's business but his and China's. That's what he'd told his attorney, Mrs. Teagues, and his mother and her boyfriend, Howard, and he'd told them over and over again: "*I didn't do anything wrong.*" Even if it was alive, and it was, he knew in his heart that it was, even before the state prosecutor presented evidence of blunt-force trauma and death by asphyxiation and exposure, it didn't matter, or shouldn't have mattered. There was no baby. There was nothing but a mistake, a mistake clothed in blood and mucus. When he really thought about it, thought it through on its merits and dissected all his mother's pathetic arguments about where he'd be today if she'd felt as he did when she was pregnant herself, he hardened like a rock, like sand turning to stone under all the pressure the planet can bring to bear. Another unwanted child in an overpopulated world? They should have given him a medal.

It was the end of January before bail was set—three hundred and fifty thousand dollars his mother didn't have—and he was released to house arrest. He wore a plastic anklet that set off an alarm if he went out the door, and so did she, so did China, imprisoned like some fairy-tale princess at her parents' house. At first, she called him every day, but mostly what she did was cry—"I want to see it," she sobbed. "I want to see our daughter's *grave*." That froze him inside. He tried to picture her—her now, China, the love of his life—and he couldn't. What did she look like? What was her face like, her nose, her hair, her eyes and breasts and the slit between her legs? He drew a blank. There was no way to summon her the way she used to be or even the way she was in court, because all he could remember was the thing that had come out of her, four limbs and the equipment of a female, shoulders rigid and eyes shut tight, as if she were a mummy in a tomb . . . and the breath, the shuddering long gasping rattle of a breath he could feel ringing inside her even as the black plastic bag closed over her face and the lid of the Dumpster opened like a mouth.

He was in the den, watching basketball, a drink in his hand (7UP mixed with Jack Daniel's in a ceramic mug, so no one would know he was getting shit-faced at two o'clock on a Sunday afternoon), when the phone rang. It was Sarah Teagues. "Listen, Jeremy," she said in her crisp, equitable tones, "I thought you ought to know—the Berkowitzes are filing a motion to have the case against China dropped."

His mother's voice on the portable, too loud, a blast of amplified breath and static: "On what grounds?"

"She never saw the baby, that's what they're saying. She thought she had a miscarriage."

"Yeah, right," his mother said.

Sarah Teagues was right there, her voice as clear and present as his mother's. "Jeremy's the one that threw it in the Dumpster, and they're saying he acted alone. She took a polygraph test day before yesterday."

He could feel his heart pounding the way it used to when he plodded up that last agonizing ridge behind the school with the cross-country team, his legs sapped, no more breath left in his body. He didn't say a word. Didn't even breathe.

"She's going to testify against him."

Outside was the world, puddles of ice clinging to the lawn under a weak afternoon sun, all the trees stripped bare, the grass dead, the azalea under the window reduced to an armload of dead brown twigs. She wouldn't have wanted to go out today anyway. This was the time of year she hated most, the long interval between the holidays and spring break, when nothing grew and nothing changed—it didn't even seem to snow much anymore. What was out there for her anyway? They wouldn't let her see Jeremy, wouldn't even let her talk to him on the phone or write him anymore, and she wouldn't be able to show her face at the mall or even the movie theater without somebody shouting out her name as if she was a freak, as if she was another Monica Lewinsky or Heidi Fleiss. She wasn't China Berkowitz, honor student, not anymore—she was the punch line to a joke, a footnote to history.

She wouldn't mind going for a drive, though—that was something she missed, just following the curves out to the reservoir to watch the way the ice cupped the shore, or up to the turnout on Route 9 to look out over the river where it oozed through the mountains in a shimmering coil of light. Or to take a walk in the woods, just that. She was in her room, on her bed, posters of bands she'd outgrown staring down from the walls, her high-school books on two shelves in the corner, the closet door flung open on all the clothes she'd once wanted so desperately she could have died for each individual pair of boots or the cashmere sweaters that felt so good against her skin. At the bottom of her left leg, down there at the foot of the bed, was the anklet she wore now, the plastic anklet with the transmitter inside, no different, she supposed, from the collars they put on wolves to track them across all those miles of barren tundra or the bears sleeping in their dens. Except that hers had an alarm on it.

For a long while she just lay there gazing out the window, watching the rinsed-out sun slip down into the sky that had no more color in it than a TV tuned to an unsubscribed channel, and then she found herself picturing things the way they were an eon ago, when everything was green. She saw the azalea bush in bloom, the leaves knifing out of the trees, butterflies—or were they cabbage moths?—hovering over the flowers. Deep green. That was the color of the world. And she was remembering a night, summer before last, just after she and Jeremy started going together, the crickets thrumming, the air thick with humidity, and him singing along with the car radio, his voice so sweet and pure it was as if he'd written the song himself, just for her. And when they got to where they were going, at the end of that dark lane overhung with trees, to a place where it was private and hushed and the night fell in on itself as if it couldn't support the weight of the stars, he was as nervous as she was. She moved into his arms, and they kissed, his lips groping for hers in the dark, his fingers trembling over the thin yielding silk of her blouse. He was Jeremy. He was the love of her life. And she closed her eyes and clung to him as if that were all that mattered.

(1999)

ACHATES McNEIL

My father is a writer. A pretty well-known one too. You'd recognize the name if I mentioned it, but I won't mention it, I'm tired of mentioning it—every time I mention it I feel as if I'm suffocating, as if I'm in a burrow deep in the ground and all these fine grains of dirt are raining down on me. We studied him in school, in the tenth grade, a story of his in one of those all-purpose anthologies that dislocate your wrists and throw out your back just to lift them from the table, and then again this year, my freshman year, in college. I got into a Contemporary American Lit class second semester and they were doing two of his novels, along with a three-page list of novels and collections by his contemporaries, and I knew some of them too—or at least I'd seen them at the house. I kept my mouth shut though, especially after the professor, this blond poet in her thirties who once wrote a novel about a nymphomaniac pastry maker, made a joke the first day when she came to my name in the register.

"Achates McNeil," she called out.

"Here," I said, feeling hot and cold all over, as if I'd gone from a sauna into a snowbank and back again. I knew what was coming; I'd been through it before.

She paused, looking up from her list to gaze out the window on the frozen wastes of the campus in the frozen skullcap of New York

State, and then came back to me and held my eyes a minute. "You wouldn't happen by any chance to be a relation of anybody on our reading list, would you?"

I sat cramped in the hard wooden seat, thinking about the faceless legions who'd sat there before me, people who'd squirmed over exams and unfeeling professorial remarks and then gone on to become plastic surgeons, gas station attendants, insurance salesmen, bums, and corpses. "No," I said. "I don't think so."

She gave me a mysterious little smile. "I was thinking of Teresa Golub or maybe Irving Thalamus?" It was a joke. One or two of the literary cretins in back gave it a nervous snort and chuckle, and I began to wonder, not for the first time, if I was really cut out for academic life. This got me thinking about the various careers available to me as a college dropout—rock and roller, chairman of the board, center for the New York Knicks—and I missed the next couple of names, coming back to the world as the name Victoria Roethke descended on the room and hung in the air like the aftershock of a detonation in the upper atmosphere.

She was sitting two rows up from me, and all I could see was her hair, draped in a Medusan snarl of wild demi-dreadlocks over everything within a three-foot radius. Her hair was red—red as in pink rather than carrot-top—and it tended to be darker on the ends but running to the color of the stuff they line Easter baskets with up close to her scalp. She didn't say here or present or yes or even nod her amazing head. She just cleared her throat and announced, "He was my grandfather."

I stopped her in the hallway after class and saw that she had all the usual equipment as well as a nose ring and two eyes the color of the cardboard stiffeners you get as a consolation prize when you have to buy a new shirt. "Are you really—?" I began, thinking we had a lot in common, thinking we could commiserate, drown our sorrows together, have sex, whatever, but before I could finish the question, she said, "No, not really."

"You mean you—?"

"That's right."

I gave her a look of naked admiration. And she was looking at me, sly and composed, looking right into my eyes. "But aren't you afraid you're going to be on Professor What's-Her-Face's shitlist when she finds out?" I said finally.

Victoria was still looking right into me. She fiddled with her hair, touched her nose ring, and gave it a quick squeeze with a nervous flutter of her fingers. Her fingernails, I saw, were painted black. "Who's going to tell her?" she said.

We were complicitous. Instantly. Half a beat later she asked me if I wanted to buy her a cup of ramen noodles in the Student Union, and I said yeah, I did, as if it was something I had any choice about.

We ran through a crust of dead snow in a stiff wind and temperatures that hadn't risen above minus ten in the past two weeks, and there were a lot of people running with us, a whole thundering herd—up here everybody ran everywhere; it was a question of survival.

In the Union she shook out her hair, and five minutes after we'd found a table in the corner and poured the hot water into the Styrofoam containers of dehydrated mystery food I could still smell the cold she'd trapped there. Otherwise I smelled the multilayered festering odors of the place, generic to college cafeterias worldwide: coffee, twice-worn underwear, cream of tomato soup. If they enclosed the place in plastic and sealed it like a tomb, it'd smell the same two thousand years from now. I'd never been in the kitchen, but I remembered the kitchen from elementary school, with its big aluminum pots and microwave ovens and all the rest, and pictured them back there now, the cafeteria ladies with their dyed hair and their miserable small-town loutish husband lives, boiling up big cauldrons of cream of tomato soup. Victoria's nose was white from the cold, but right where the nose ring plunged in, over the flange of her left nostril, there was a spot of flesh as pink as the ends of her hair.

"What happens when you get a cold?" I said. "I mean, I've always wondered."

She was blowing into her noodles, and she looked up to shoot me a quick glance out of her cardboard eyes. Her mouth was small, her teeth the size of individual kernels of niblet corn. When she smiled, as she did now, she showed acres of gum. "It's a pain in the ass." Half a beat: that was her method. "I suffer it all for beauty."

And of course this is where I got all gallant and silver-tongued and told her how striking it was, she was, her hair and her eyes and— but she cut me off. "You really are his son, aren't you?" she said.

There was a sudden eruption of jocklike noises from the far end of the room—some athletes with shaved heads making sure everybody knew they were there—and it gave me a minute to compose myself, aside from blowing into my noodles and adjusting my black watch cap with the Yankees logo for the fourteenth time, that is. I shrugged. Looked into her eyes and away again. "I really don't want to talk about it."

But she was on her feet suddenly and people were staring at her and there was a look on her face like she'd just won the lottery or the trip for two to the luxurious Spermata Inn on the beach at Waikiki. "I don't believe it," she said, and her voice was as deep as mine, strange really, but with a just detectable breathiness or hollowness to it that made it recognizably feminine.

I was holding on to my Styrofoam container of hot noodles as if somebody was trying to snatch it away from me. A quick glance from side to side reassured me that the people around us had lost interest, absorbed once again in their plates of reheated stir-fry, newspapers, and cherry Cokes. I gave her a weak smile.

"You mean, you're like really Tom McNeil's son, no bullshit?"

"Yes," I said, and though I liked the look of her, of her breasts clamped in the neat interwoven grid of a blue thermal undershirt and her little mouth and the menagerie of her hair, and I liked what she'd done in class too, my voice was cold. "And I have a whole other life too."

But she wasn't listening. "Oh, my God!" she squealed, ignoring the sarcasm and all it was meant to imply. She did something with her hands, her face; her hair helicoptered round her head. "I can't believe it. He's my hero, he's my god. I want to have his baby!"

The noodles congealed in my mouth like wet confetti. I didn't have the heart to point out that I *was* his baby, for better or worse.

It wasn't that I hated him exactly—it was far more complicated than that, and I guess it got pretty Freudian too, considering the way he treated my mother and the fact that I was thirteen and having problems of my own when he went out the door like a big cliché and my mother collapsed into herself as if her bones had suddenly melted. I'd seen him maybe three or four times since and always with some woman or other and a fistful of money and a face that looked like he'd just got done licking up a pile of dogshit off the sidewalk. What did he want from me? What did he expect? At least he'd waited till my sister and brother were in college, at least they were out of the house when the cleaver fell, but what about me? I was the one who had to go into that classroom in the tenth grade and read that shitty story and have the teacher look at me like I had something to share, some intimate little anecdote I could relate about what it was like living with a genius—or having lived with a genius. And I was the one who had to see his face all over the newspapers and magazines when he published *Blood Ties*, his postmodernist take on the breakdown of the family, a comedy no less, and then read in the interviews about how his wife and children had held him back and stifled him— as if we were his jailers or something. As if I'd ever bothered him or dared to approach the sanctum of his upstairs office when his genius was percolating or asked him to go to a Little League game and sit in the stands and yabber along with the rest of the parents. Not me. No, I was the dutiful son of the big celebrity, and the funny thing was, I wouldn't have even known he was a celebrity if he hadn't packed up and left.

He was my father. A skinny man in his late forties with kinky hair and a goatee who dressed like he was twenty-five and had a dead black morbid outlook on life and twisted everything into the kind of joke that made you squirm. I was proud of him. I loved him. But then I saw what a monster of ego he was, as if anybody could give two shits for literature anymore, as if he was the center of the universe while the real universe went on in the streets, on the Internet, on TV, and in the movie theaters. Who the hell was he to reject me?

So: Victoria Roethke.

I told her I'd never licked anybody's nose ring before and she asked me if I wanted to go over to her apartment and listen to music and have sex, and though I felt like shit, like my father's son, like the negative image of something I didn't want to be, I went. Oh, yes: I went.

She lived in a cramped drafty ancient wreck of a nondescript house from the wood-burning era, about five blocks from campus. We ran all the way, of course—it was either that or freeze to the pavement—and the shared effort, the wheezing lungs and burning nostrils, got us over any awkwardness that might have ensued. We stood a minute in the superheated entryway that featured a row of tarnished brass coathooks, a dim hallway lined with doors coated in drab shiny paint and a smell of cat litter and old clothes. I followed her hair up a narrow stairway and into a one-room apartment not much bigger than a prison cell. It was dominated by a queen-size mattress laid out on the floor and a pair of speakers big enough to double as end tables, which they did. Bricks and boards for the bookcases that lined the walls and pinched them in like one of those shrinking rooms in a sci-fi flick, posters to cover up the faded nineteenth-century wallpaper, a greenish-looking aquarium with one pale bloated fish suspended like a mobile in the middle of it. The solitary window looked out on everything that was dead in the world. Bathroom down the hall.

And what did her room smell like? Like an animal's den, like a burrow or a hive. And female. Intensely female. I glanced at the pile of brassieres, panties, body stockings, and sweatsocks in the corner, and she lit a joss stick, pulled the curtains, and put on a CD by a band I don't want to name here, but which I like—there was no problem with her taste or anything like that. Or so I thought.

She straightened up from bending over the CD player and turned to me in the half-light of the curtained room and said, "You like this band?"

We were standing there like strangers amidst the intensely personal detritus of her room, awkward and insecure. I didn't know her. I'd never been there before. And I must have seemed like some weird growth sprung up on the unsuspecting flank of her personal space. "Yeah," I said, "they're hot," and I was going to expand on that with some technical praise, just to let her see how hip and knowing I was, when she threw out a sigh and let her arms fall to her sides.

"I don't know," she said, "what I really like is soul and gospel—especially gospel. I put this on for you."

I felt deflated suddenly, unhip and uncool. There she was, joss stick sweetening the air, her hair a world of its own, my father's fan—my absent famous self-absorbed son of a bitch of a father actually pimping for me—and I didn't know what to say. After an awkward pause, the familiar band slamming down their chords and yowling out their shopworn angst, I said, "Let's hear some of your stuff then."

She looked pleased, her too-small mouth pushed up into something resembling a smile, and then she stepped forward and enveloped me in her hair. We kissed. She kissed me, actually, and I responded, and then she bounced the two steps to the CD player and put on Berna Berne and the Angeline Sisters, a slow thump of tinny drums and an organ that sounded like something fresh out of the muffler shop, followed by a high-pitched blur of semihysterical voices. "Like it?" she said.

What could I say? "It's different," I said.

She assured me it would grow on me, like anything else, if I gave it half a chance, ran down the other band for their pedestrian posturing, and invited me to get into her bed. "But don't take off your clothes," she said, "not yet."

I had a three o'clock class in psychology, the first meeting of the semester, and I suspected I was going to miss it. I was right. Victoria made a real ritual of the whole thing, clothes coming off with the masturbatory dalliance of a strip show, the covers rolling back periodically to show this patch of flesh or that, strategically revealed. I discovered her breasts one at a time, admired the tattoo on her ankle (a backward *S* that proved, according to her, that she was a reincarnated Norse skald), and saw that she really was a redhead in the conventional sense. Her lips were dry, her tongue was unstoppable, her hair a primal encounter. When we were done, she sat up and I saw that her breasts pointed in two different directions, and that was human in a way I can't really express, a very personal thing, as if she was letting me in on a secret that was more intimate than the sex itself. I was touched. I admit it. I looked at those mismatched breasts and they meant more to me than her lips and her eyes and the deep thrumming instrument of her voice, if you know what I mean.

"So," she said, sipping from a mug of water she produced from somewhere amongst a stack of books and papers scattered beside the mattress, "what do I call you? I mean, Achates—right?—that's a real mouthful."

"That's my father," I said. "One of his bullshit affectations—how could the great one have a kid called Joe or Evan or Jim-Bob or Dickie?" My head was on the pillow, my eyes were on the ceiling. "You know what my name means? It means 'faithful companion,' can you believe that?"

She was silent a moment, her gray eyes locked on me over the lip of the cup, her breasts dimpling with the cold. "Yeah," she said, "I can see what you mean," and she pulled the covers up to her throat. "But what do people call you?"

I stared bleakly across the room, fastening on nothing, and when I exhaled I could see my breath. Berna Berne and the Angeline Sisters were still at it, punishing the rhythm section and charging after the vocals till you'd think somebody had set their dresses on fire. "My father calls me Ake," I said finally, "or at least he used to when I used to know him. And in case you're wondering how you spell that, that's Ake with a *k*."

Victoria dropped out of the blond poet-novelist's Lit class, but I knew where she lived and you couldn't miss her hair jogging across the tundra. I saw her maybe two or three times a week, especially on weekends. When things began to get to me—life, exams, too many shooters of Jack or tequila, my mother's zombielike voice on the telephone—I sank into the den of Victoria's room with its animal funk and shrinking walls as if I'd never climb back out, and it was nothing like the cold, dry burrow I thought of when I thought of my father. Just the opposite: Victoria's room, with Victoria in it, was positively tropical, whether you could see your breath or not. I even began to develop a tolerance for the Angeline Sisters.

I avoided class the day we dissected the McNeil canon, but I was there for Delmore Schwartz and his amazing re-creation of his parents' courtship unfolding on a movie screen in his head. In dreams begin responsibilities—yes, sure, but whose responsibility was I? And how long would I have to wait before we got to the sequel and *my* dreams? I'd looked through the photo albums, my mother an open-faced hippie in cutoffs and serape with her seamless blond hair and Slavic cheekbones and my father cocky and staring into the lens out of the shining halo of his hair, everything a performance, even a simple photograph, even then. The sperm and the egg, that was a biological concept, that was something I could envision up there on the big screen, the wriggling clot of life, the wet glowing ball of the egg, but picturing them coming together, his coldness, his arrogance, his total absorption in himself, that was beyond me. Chalk it up to reticence. To DNA. To the grandiosity of the patriarchal cock. But then he was me and I was him and how else could you account for it?

It was Victoria who called my attention to the poster. The posters, that is, about six million of them plastered all over every stationary object within a two-mile orbit of the campus as if he was a rock star or something, as if he really counted for anything, as if anybody could even read anymore let alone give half a shit about a balding, leather-jacketed, ex-hippie wordmeister who worried about his image first, his groin second, and nothing else after that. How did I miss it? A nearsighted dwarf couldn't have missed it—in fact, all the nearsighted dwarves on campus had already seen it and were lining up with everybody even vaguely ambulatory for their $2.50 Student Activities Board–sponsored tickets:

TOM MCNEIL
READING FROM ELECTRONIC
ORPHANS & BLOOD TIES
FEB. 28, 8:00 P.M.
DUBOFSKY HALL

Victoria was right there with me, out front of the Student Union, the poster with his mug shot of a photo staring out at me from behind the double-insulated glass panel that reflected the whole dead Arctic world and me in the middle of it, and we had to dance on our toes and do aerobics for a full two minutes there to stave off hypothermia while I let the full meaning of it sink in. My first response was outrage, and so was my second. I bundled Victoria through the door and out of the blast of the cold, intimately involved in the revolution of her hair, the smell of her gray bristling fake fur coat that looked like half a dozen opossums dropped on her from high, even the feel of her breasts beneath all that wintry armament, and I howled in protest.

"How in Christ's name could he do this to me?" I shouted across the echoing entranceway, pink-nosed idiots in their hooded parkas coming and going, giving me their eat-shit-and-die looks. I was furious, out of control. Victoria snatched at my arm to calm me, but I tore away from her.

"He planned this, you know. He had to. He couldn't leave well enough alone, couldn't let me get away from him and be just plain nobody up here amongst the cowflops in this podunk excuse for a university—no, it's not Harvard, it's not Stanford, but at least I didn't take a nickel of his money for it. You think he'd ever even consider reading here even if the Board of Regents got down and licked his armpits and bought him a new Porsche and promised him all the coeds in Burge to fuck one by one till they dropped dead from the sheer joy of it?"

Victoria just stood there looking at me out of her flat gray eyes, rocking back and forth on the heels of her red leather boots with the cowgirl filigree. We were blocking the doors and people were tramping in and out, passing between us, a trail of yellow slush dribbling behind them in either direction. "I don't know," Victoria said over the heads of two Asian girls wrapped up like corpses, "I think it's kind of cool."

A day later, the letter came. Personalized stationery, California address. I tore it open in the hallway outside the door of my overheated, overlit, third-floor room in the sad-smelling old dorm:

Querido Ake:

I know it's been a while but my crazy life just gets crazier what with the European tour for *Orphans* and Judy and Josh, but I want to make it up to you however I can. I asked Jules to get me the gig at Acadia purposely to give me an excuse to see how you're getting along. Let's do dinner or something afterward—bring one of your girlfriends along. We'll do it up. We will.

Mucho,
Dad

This hit me like a body blow in the late rounds of a prizefight. I was already staggering, bloodied from a hundred hooks and jabs, ten to one against making it to the bell, and now this. Boom. I sat down on my institutional bed and read the thing over twice. Judy was his new wife, and Josh, six months old and still shitting in his pants, was my new brother. Half brother. DNA rules. Shit, it would have been funny if he was dead and I was dead and the whole world a burnt-out cinder floating in the dead-black hole of the universe. But I wasn't dead, and didn't want to be, not yet at least. The next best thing was being drunk, and that was easy to accomplish. Three Happy Hours and a good lip-splitting, sideburn-thumping altercation with some mountainous asshole in a pair of Revo shades later, and I was ready for him.

You probably expect me to report that my father, the genius, blew into town and fucked my Lit professor, Victoria, the cafeteria ladies, and two or three dogs he stumbled across on the way to the reading, but that's not the way it fell out. Not at all. In fact, he was kind of sorry and subdued and old-looking. Real old-looking, though by my count he must have been fifty-three or maybe fifty-four. It was as if his whole head had collapsed like a rotten jack-o'-lantern, his eyes sucked down these volcanoes of wrinkles, his hair standing straight up on his head like a used toilet brush. But I'm getting ahead of myself. According to my roommate, Jeff Heymann, he'd called about a hundred times and finally left a message saying he was coming in early and wanted to have lunch too, if that was okay with me. It wasn't okay. I stayed away from the telephone, and I stayed away from my room. In fact, I didn't even go near the campus for fear of running into him as he long-legged his way across the quad, entourage in tow. I blew off my classes and sank into Victoria's nest as if it was an opium den, sleep and forgetfulness, Berna Berne and the Angeline Sisters keeping me company, along with a bottle of Don Q Victoria's dad had brought back from Puerto Rico for her.

What was my plan? To crash and burn. To get so fucked up I'd be in a demi-coma till the lunch was eaten, the reading read and dinner forgotten. I mean, fuck him. Really.

The fatal flaw in my plan was Victoria.

She didn't stay there to comfort me with her hair, her neat little zipper of a mouth, and her mismatched breasts. No, she went to class, very big day, exams and papers and quizzes. So she said. But do I have to tell you where she really was? Can't you picture it? The fan, the diehard, somebody who supposedly cared about me, and there she was, camped outside his hotel in the Arctic wind with the snot crusted round her nose ring. They wouldn't tell her what room he was in, and when she took exception to the attitude of the girl behind the desk, they told her she'd have to wait outside—on the public sidewalk. While she was waiting and freezing and I was attempting to drink myself comatose, he was making phone calls. Another hundred to my room and then to the registrar and the dean and anybody else who might have had a glimmer of my whereabouts, and of course they all fell over dead and contacted my professors, the local police—Christ, probably even the FBI, the CIA, and TRW.

And then it was lunchtime and all the cheeses and honchos from the English Department wanted to break bread with him, so out the door he went, not with Judy on his arm or some more casual acquaintance who might have been last night's groin mas-sager or the flight attendant who'd served him his breakfast, but his biographer. His biographer. Arm in arm with this bald guy half his height and a face depleted by a pair of glasses the size of the ones Elton John used to wear onstage, trailing dignitaries and toadies, and who does he run into?

Ten minutes later he's coming up the stairs at Victoria's place, and beneath the wailing of the Sisters and the thump of the organ I can hear his footsteps, his and nobody else's, and I know this: after all these years my father has come for me.

■ ■ ■

Lunch was at the Bistro, one of the few places in town that aspired to anything more than pizza, burgers, and burritos. My father sat at the head of the table, of course, and I, three-quarters drunk on white rum, sat at his right hand. Victoria was next to me, her expression rapt, her hair snaking out behind me in the direction of the great man like the tendrils of some unkillable plant, and the biographer, sunk behind his glasses, hunched beside her with a little black notepad. The rest of the table, from my father's side down, was occupied by various members of the English Department I vaguely recognized and older lawyer types who must have been deans or whatever. There was an awkward moment when Dr. Delpino, my American Lit professor, came in, but her eyes, after registering the initial surprise and recalculating our entire relationship from the first day's roll call on, showed nothing but a sort of fawning, shimmering awe. And how did I feel about that? Sick. Just plain sick.

I drank desperate cups of black coffee and tried to detoxify myself with something called Coquilles Saint Jacques, which amounted to an indefinable rubbery substance sealed in an impenetrable layer of baked cheese. My father held forth, witty, charming, as pleased with himself as anybody alive. He said things like "I'm glad you're asking me to speak on the only subject I'm an authority on—me," and with every other breath he dropped the names of the big impressive actors who'd starred in the big impressive movie version of his last book. "Well," he'd say, "as far as that goes, Meryl once told me . . . ," or, "When we were on location in Barbados, Brad and Geena and I used to go snorkeling practically every afternoon, and then it was conch ceviche and this rum drink they call Mata-Mata, after the turtle, and believe me, kill you it does. . . ."

Add to this the fact that he kept throwing his arm round the back of my chair (and so, my shoulders) as if I'd been there with him through every scintillating tête-à-tête and sexual and literary score, and you might begin to appreciate how I felt. But what could I do?

He was playing a role that would have put to shame any of the big-gun actors he named, and I was playing my role too, and though I was seething inside, though I felt betrayed by Victoria and him and all the stupid noshing doglike faces fawning round the table, I played the dutiful and proud son to Academy Award proportions. Or maybe I wasn't so great. At least I didn't jump up and flip the table over and call him a fraud, a cheat, and a philanderer who had no right to call anybody his son, let alone me. But oh, how those deans and professors sidled up to me afterward to thoroughly kiss my ass while Dr. Delpino glowed over our little secret and tried to shoulder Victoria out of the way. And Victoria. That was another thing. Victoria didn't seem to recall that I was still alive, so enthralled was she by the overblown spectacle of my father the genius.

He took me aside just before we stepped back out into the blast of the wind, confidential and fatherly, the others peeling back momentarily in deference to the ties of the blood, and asked me if I was all right. "Are you all right?" he said.

Everything was in a stir, crescendoing voices, the merry ritual of the zippers, the gloves, the scarves and parkas, a string quartet keening through the speakers in some weird key that made the hair stand up on the back of my neck. "What do you mean?" I said.

I looked into his face then, and the oldness dropped away from him: he was my pal, my dad, the quick-blooded figure I remembered from the kitchen, den, and bedroom of my youth. "I don't know," he said, shrugging. "Victoria said—that's her name, right, Victoria?"

I nodded.

"She said you were feeling sick, the flu or something," and he let it trail off. Somebody shouted, "You should have seen it in December!" and the string quartet choked off in an insectlike murmur of busy strings and nervous fingers. "Cute kid, Victoria," he said. "She's something." And then a stab at a joke: "Guess you inherited my taste, huh?"

But the dutiful son didn't smile, let alone laugh. He was feeling less like Achates than Oedipus.

"You need any money?" my father said, and he was reaching into the pocket of his jeans, an automatic gesture, when the rest of the group converged on us and the question fell dead. He threw an arm round me suddenly and managed to snag Victoria and the proud flag of her hair in the other. He gave a two-way squeeze with his skinny arms and said, "See you at the reading tonight, right?"

Everyone was watching, right on down to the busboys, not to mention the biographer, Dr. Delpino, and all the by-now stunned, awed, and grinning strangers squinting up from their coquilles and fritures. It was a real biographical moment. "Yeah," I said, and I thought for a minute they were going to break into applause, "sure."

The hall was packed, standing room only, hot and stifled with the crush of bodies and the coats and scarves and other paraphernalia that were like a second shadowy crowd gathered at the edges of the living and breathing one, students, faculty, and townspeople wedged into every available space. Some of them had come from as far away as Vermont and Montreal, so I heard, and when we came through the big main double doors, scalpers were selling the $2.50 Student Activities Board–sponsored tickets for three and four times face value. I sat in the front row between my father's vacant seat and the biographer (whose name was Mal, as in Malcolm) while my father made the rounds, pumping hands and signing books, napkins, sheets of notebook paper, and whatever else the adoring crowd thrust at him. Victoria, the mass of her hair enlarged to even more stupendous proportions thanks to some mysterious chemical treatment she'd undergone in the bathroom down the hall from her room, sat sprouting beside me.

I was trying not to watch my father, plunging in and out of the jungle of Victoria to make small talk, unconcerned, unflappable, no problem at all, when Mal leaned across the vacant seat and poked my arm with the butt of his always handy Scripto pen. I turned to him, Victoria's hand clutched tightly in mine—she hadn't let go, not even to unwrap her scarf, since we'd climbed out of the car—and stared into the reflected blaze of his glasses. They were amazing, those glasses, like picture windows, like a scuba mask grafted to his hairless skull. "Nineteen eighty-nine," he said, "when he wrecked the car? The BMW, I mean?" I sat there frozen, waiting for the rest of it, the man's voice snaking into my consciousness till it felt like the voice of my innermost self. "Do you remember if he was still living at home then? Or was that after he . . . after he, uh, moved out?"

Moved out. Wrecked the car.

"Do you remember what he was like then? Were there any obvious changes? Did he seem depressed?"

He must have seen from my face how I felt about the situation because his glasses suddenly flashed light, he tugged twice at his lower lip, and murmured, "I know this isn't the time or place, I was just curious, that's all. But I wonder, would you mind—maybe we could set up a time to talk?"

What could I say? Victoria clutched my hand like a trophy hunter, my fellow students rumbled and chattered and stretched in their bolted-down seats, and my father squatted here, sprang up there, lifted his eyebrows, and laid down a layer of witty banter about half a mile thick. I shrugged. Looked away. "Sure," I said.

Then the lights dimmed once, twice, and went all the way down, and the chairman of the English Department took the podium while my father scuttled into the seat beside me and the audience hushed. I won't bother describing the chairman—he was generic, and he talked for a mercifully short five minutes or so about how my father needed no introduction and et cetera, et cetera, before giving the podium over to Mal, as in Malcolm, the official hagiographer. Mal bounced up onto the stage like a trained seal, and if the chairman was selfless and brief, Mal was windy, verbose, a man who really craved an audience. He softened them up with half a dozen anecdotes about the great man's hyperinflated past, with carefully selected references to drug abuse, womanizing, unhinged driving, and of course movies and movie stars. By the time he was done he'd made my father sound like a combination of James Dean, Tolstoy, and Enzo Ferrari. They were thrilled, every last man, woman, and drooling freshman—and me, the only one in the audience who really knew him? I wanted to puke, puke till the auditorium was filled to the balcony, puke till they were swimming in it. But I couldn't. I was trapped, just like in some nightmare. Right there in the middle of the front row.

When Mal finally ducked his denuded head and announced my father, the applause was seismic, as if the whole auditorium had been tipped on end, and the great man, in one of his own tour T-shirts and the omnipresent leather jacket, took the stage and engaged in a little high-fiving with the departing biographer while the thunder gradually subsided and the faces round me went slack with wonder. For the next fifteen minutes he pranced and strutted across the stage, ignoring the podium and delivering a preprogrammed monologue that was the equal of anything you'd see on late-night TV. At least all the morons around me thought so. He charmed them, out-hipped them, and they laughed, snorted, sniggered, and howled. Some of them, my fellow freshmen, no doubt, even stamped their feet in thunderous unison as if they were at a pep rally or something. And the jokes—the sort of thing he'd come on with at lunch—were all so self-effacing, at least on the surface, but deep down each phrase and buttressed pause was calculated to remind us we were in the presence of one of the heroes of literature. There was the drinking-with-Bukowski story, which had been reproduced in every interview he'd done in the last twenty years, the traveling-through-Russia-with-nothing-but-a-pair-of-jeans-two-socks-and-a-leather-jacket-after-his-luggage-was-stolen story, the obligatory movie star story, and three or four don't-ask-me-now references to his wild past. I sat there like a condemned man awaiting the lethal injection, a rigid smile frozen to my face. My scalp itched, both nostrils, even the crotch of my underwear. I fought for control.

And then the final blow fell, as swift and sudden as a meteor shrieking down from outer space and against all odds blasting through the roof of the auditorium and drilling right into the back of my reeling head. My father raised a hand to indicate that the jokes were over, and the audience choked off as if he'd tightened a noose around each and every throat. Suddenly he was more professorial than the professors—there wasn't a murmur in the house, not even a cough. He held up a book, produced a pair of wire-rim glasses—a prop if ever I saw one—and glanced down at me. "The piece I want to read tonight, from *Blood Ties*, is something I've wanted to read in public for a long time. It's a deeply personal piece, and painful too, but I read it tonight as an act of contrition. I read it for my son."

He spread open the book with a slow, sad deliberation I'm sure they all found very affecting, but to me he was like a terrorist opening a suitcase full of explosives, and I shrank into my seat, as miserable as I've ever been in my life. He can't be doing this, I thought, he can't. But he was. It was his show, after all.

And then he began to read. At first I didn't hear the words, didn't want to—I was in a daze, mesmerized by the intense weirdness of his voice, which had gone high-pitched and nasal all of a sudden, with a kind of fractured rhythm that made it seem as if he was translating from another language. It took me a moment, and then I understood: this was his reading voice, another affectation. Once I got past that, there were the words themselves, each one a little missile aimed at me, the hapless son, the victim who only wanted to be left lying in the wreckage where he'd fallen. He was reading a passage in which the guilt-racked but lusty father takes the fourteen-year-old son out to the best restaurant in town for a heart-to-heart talk about those lusts, about dreams, responsibilities, and the domestic life that was dragging him down. I tried to close myself off, but I couldn't. My eyes were burning. Nobody in the auditorium was watching him anymore—how could they be? No, they were watching me. Watching the back of my head. Watching the fiction come to life.

I did the only thing I could. When he got to the part where the son, tears streaming into his chocolate mousse, asks him why, why, Dad, why, I stood up, right there, right in the middle of the front row, all those eyes drilling into me. I tore my hand away from Victoria's, stared down the biographer and Dr. Delpino and all the rest of them, and stalked straight out the nearest exit even as my father's amplified voice wavered, faltered, and then came back strong again, nothing wrong, nothing the matter, nothing a little literature wouldn't cure.

I don't know what happened between him and Victoria at the muted and minimally celebratory dinner later that night, but I don't suspect it was much, if anything. That wasn't the problem, and both of us—she and I, that is—knew it. I spent the night hiding out in the twenty-four-hour Laundromat wedged between Brewskies Pub and Taco Bell, and in the morning I ate breakfast in a greasy spoon only the townies frequented and then caught up on some of Hollywood's distinguished product at the local cineplex for as long as I could stand it. By then, I was sure the great man would have gone on to his many other great appointments, all his public posturing aside. And that was just what happened: he canceled his first flight and hung around till he could hang around no longer, flying out at four-fifteen with his biographer and all the sympathy of the deeply yearning and heartbroken campus. And me? I was nobody again. Or so I thought.

I too dropped out of Dr. Delpino's class—I couldn't stand the thought of that glazed blue look of accusation in her eyes—and though I occasionally spotted Victoria's hair riding the currents around campus, I avoided her. She knew where to find me if she wanted me, but all that was over, I could see that—I wasn't his son after all. A few weeks later I noticed her in the company of this senior who played keyboards in one of the local bands, and I felt something, I don't know what it was, but it wasn't jealousy. And then, at the end of a lonely semester in a lonely town in the lonely hind end of nowhere, the air began to soften and a few blades of yellow grass poked up through the rotting snow and my roommate took me downtown to Brewskies to celebrate.

The girl's name was Marlene, but she didn't pronounce it like the old German actress who was probably dead before she was born, but Mar-*lenna*, the second syllable banged out till it sounded as if she was calling herself Lenny. I liked the way her smile showed off the gold caps on her molars. The band I didn't want to mention earlier was playing through the big speakers over the bar, and there was a whole undercurrent of noise and excitement mixed with the smells of tap beer, Polish sausage, and salt-and-vinegar chips. "I know you," she said. "You're, um, Tom McNeil's son, right?"

I never looked away from her, never blinked. All that was old news now, dead and buried, like some battle in the Civil War.

"That's right," I said. "How did you guess?"

(1995)

56–0

It wasn't the cast that bothered him—the thing was like rock, like a weapon, and that was just how he would use it—and it wasn't the hyperextended knee or the hip pointer or the yellowing contusions seeping into his thighs and hams and lower back or even the gouged eye that was swollen shut and drooling a thin pale liquid the color of dishwater; no, it was the humiliation. Fifty-six to nothing. That was no mere defeat; it was a drubbing, an ass-kicking, a rape, the kind of thing the statisticians and sports nerds would snigger over as long as there were records to keep. He'd always felt bigger than life in his pads and helmet, a hero, a titan, but you couldn't muster much heroism lying facedown in the mud at fifty-six to nothing and with the other team's third string in there. No, the cast didn't bother him, not really, though it itched like hell and his hand was a big stippled piece of meat sticking out of the end of it, or the eye either, though it was ugly, pure ugly. The trainer had sent him to the eye doctor and the doctor had put some kind of blue fluid in the eye and peered into it with a little conical flashlight and said there was no lasting damage, but still it was swollen shut and he couldn't study for his Physical Communications exam.

It was Sunday, the day after the game, and Ray Arthur Larry-Pete Fontinot, right guard for the Caledonia College Shuckers, slept till

two, wrapped in his own private misery—and even then he couldn't
get out of bed. Every fiber of his body, all six feet, four inches and
two hundred sixty-eight pounds of it, shrieked with pain. He was
twenty-two years old, a senior, his whole life ahead of him, and he
felt like he was ready for the nursing home. There was a ringing in
his ears, his eyelashes were welded together, his lower back throbbed,
and both his knees felt as if ice picks had been driven into them. He
hobbled, splayfooted and naked, to the bathroom at the end of the
hall, and there was blood in the toilet bowl when he was done.

All his life he'd been a slow fat pasty kid, beleaguered and tor-
mented by his quick-footed classmates, until he found his niche on
the football field, where his bulk, stubborn and immovable, had
proved an advantage—or so he'd thought. He'd drunk the protein
drink, pumped the iron, lumbered around the track like some geriatric buffalo, and what had it gotten him? Caledonia had gone 0–43
during his four years on the varsity squad, never coming closer than
two touchdowns even to a tie—and the forty-third loss had been the
hardest. Fifty-six to nothing. He'd donned a football helmet to feel
good about himself, to develop pride and poise, to taste the sweet
nectar of glory, but somehow he didn't feel all that glorious lying
there flat on his back and squinting one-eyed at Puckett and Poplar's
Principles of Physical Communications: A Text, until the lines shifted
before him like the ranks of *X*s and *O*s in the Coach's eternal dia-
grams. He dozed. Woke again to see the evening shadows closing
over the room. By nightfall, he felt good enough to get up and puke.

In the morning, a full forty hours after the game had ended, he felt
even worse, if that was possible. He sat up, goaded by the first tumul-
tuous stirrings of his gut, and winced as he pulled the sweats over
each bruised and puckered calf. His right knee locked up on him as
he angled his feet into the laceless hightops (it had been three years
at least since he'd last been able to bend down and tie his shoes),
something cried out in his left shoulder as he pulled the Caledonia

sweatshirt over his head, and then suddenly he was on his feet and ambulatory. He staggered down the hall like something out of *Night of the Living Dead*, registering a familiar face here and there, but the faces were a blur mostly, and he avoided the eyes attached to them. Someone was playing Killer Pussy at seismic volume, and someone else—some half-witted dweeb he'd gladly have murdered if only his back didn't hurt so much—had left a skateboard outside the door and Ray Arthur Larry-Pete damn near crushed it to powder and pitched right on through the concrete-block wall in the bargain, but if nothing else, he still had his reflexes. As he crossed the courtyard to the cafeteria in a lively blistering wind, he noted absently that he'd progressed from a hobble to a limp.

There was no sign of Suzie in the cafeteria, and he had a vague recollection of her calling to cancel their study date the previous evening, but as he loaded up his tray with desiccated bacon strips, mucilaginous eggs, and waffles that looked, felt, and tasted like roofing material, he spotted Kitwany, Moss, and DuBoy skulking over their plates at one of the long tables in the back of the room. It would have been hard to miss them. Cut from the same exaggerated mold as he, his fellow linemen loomed over the general run of the student body like representatives of another species. Their heads were like prize pumpkins set on the pedestals of their neckless shoulders, their fingers were the size of the average person's forearm, their jaws were entities unto themselves and they sprouted casts like weird growths all over their bodies.

Ray Arthur Larry-Pete made the long limp across the room to join them, setting his tray down gingerly and using both his hands to brace himself as he lowered his bruised backside to the unforgiving hardwood slats of the bench. Then, still employing his hands, he lifted first one and then the other deadened leg over the bench and into the well beneath the table. He grunted, winced, cursed, broke wind. Then he nodded to his teammates, worked his spine into the swallowing position and addressed himself to his food.

After a moment, DuBoy spoke. He was wearing a neck brace in the place where his head was joined to his shoulders, and it squeezed the excess flesh of his jowls up into his face so that he looked like an enormous rodent. "How you feeling?"

You didn't speak of pain. You toughed it out—that was the code. Coach Tundra had been in the army in Vietnam at some place Ray Arthur Larry-Pete could never remember or pronounce, and he didn't tolerate whiners and slackers. *Pain?* he would yelp incredulously at the first hint that a player was even thinking of staying down. *Tell it to the 101st Airborne, to the boys taking a mortar round in the Ia Drang Valley or the grunts in the field watching their buddies get blown away and then crawling six miles through a swamp so thick it would choke a snake with both their ears bleeding down their neck and their leg gone at the knee. Get up, soldier. Get out there and fight!* And if that didn't work, he'd roll up his pant leg to show off the prosthesis.

Ray Arthur Larry-Pete glanced up at DuBoy. "I'll live. How about you?"

DuBoy tried to shrug as if to say it was nothing, but even the faintest lift of a shoulder made him gasp and slap a hand to the neck brace as if a hornet had stung him. "No . . . big thing," he croaked finally.

There was no sound then but for the onomatopoeia of the alimentary process—food going in, jaws seizing it, throats closing on the load and opening again for the next—and the light trilling mealtime chatter of their fellow students, the ones unencumbered by casts and groin pulls and bloody toilets. Ray Arthur Larry-Pete was depressed. Over the loss, sure—but it went deeper than that. He was brooding about his college career, his job prospects, life after football. There was a whole winter, spring, and summer coming up in which, for the first time in as long as he could remember, he wouldn't have to worry about training for football season, and he couldn't imagine what that would be like. No locker room, no sweat, no pads, no stink of shower drains or the mentholated reek of ointment, no jock itch or aching muscles, no training table, no trainer—no chance, however slim, for glory....

And more immediately, he was fretting about his coursework. There was the Phys. Comm. exam he hadn't been able to study for, and the quiz the professor would almost certainly spring in Phys. Ed., and there were the three-paragraph papers required for both Phys. Training and Phys. Phys., and he was starting to get a little paranoid about Suzie, one of the quintessentially desirable girls on campus, with all her assets on public view, and what did he have to offer her but the glamour of football? Why had she backed out on their date? Did this mean their engagement was off, that she wanted a winner, that this was the beginning of the end?

He was so absorbed in his thoughts he didn't register what Moss was saying when he dropped his bomb into the little silence at the table. Moss was wearing a knee brace and his left arm was in a sling. He was using his right to alternately take a bite of his own food and to lift a heaping forkful from Kitwany's plate to Kitwany's waiting lips. Kitwany was in a full-shoulder harness, both arms frozen in front of him as if he were a sleepwalker cast in plaster of Paris. Ray Arthur Larry-Pete saw Moss's mouth working, but the words flew right by him. "What did you say, Moss?" he murmured, looking up from his food.

"I said Coach says we're probably going to have to forfeit to State."

Ray Arthur Larry-Pete was struck dumb. "Forfeit?" he finally gasped, and the blood was thundering in his temples. "What the hell do you mean, forfeit?"

A swirl of snow flurries scoured his unprotected ears as he limped grimly across the quad to the Phys. Ed. building, muttering under his breath. What was the Coach thinking? Didn't he realize this was the seniors' last game, their last and only chance to assuage the sting of 56–0, the final time they'd ever pull on their cleats against State,

Caledonia's bitterest rival, a team they hadn't beaten in modern historical times? Was he crazy?

It was cold, wintry, the last week in November, and Ray Arthur Larry-Pete Fontinot had to reach up with his good hand to pull his collar tight against his throat as he mounted the big concrete steps brushed with snow. The shooting hot-wire pains that accompanied this simple gesture were nothing, nothing at all, and he barely grimaced, reaching down automatically for the push-bar on the big heavy eight-foot-tall double doors. He nodded at a pair of wrestlers running the stairs in gym shorts, made his way past the woefully barren trophy case (*Caledonia College, Third Place Divisional Finish, 1938* read the inscription on the lone trophy, which featured a bronzed figurine in antiquated leather headgear atop a pedestal engraved with the scores of that lustrous long-ago 6-and-5 season, the only winning season Caledonia could boast of in any of its athletic divisions, except for women's field hockey and who counted that?), tested his knees on the third grueling flight of stairs, and approached the Coach's office by the side door. Coach Tundra almost never inhabited his official office on the main corridor, a place of tidy desks, secretaries, and seasonal decorations; of telephones, copiers, and the new lone fax machine he could use to instantaneously trade *X*s and *O*s with his colleagues at other colleges, if he so chose. No, he preferred the back room, a tiny unheated poorly lit cubicle cluttered with the detritus of nineteen unprofitable seasons. Ray Arthur Larry-Pete peered through the open doorway to find the Coach slumped over his desk, face buried in his hands. "Coach?" he said softly.

No reaction.

"Coach?"

From the nest of his hands, the Coach's rucked and gouged face gradually emerged and the glittering wicked raptor's eyes that had struck such bowel-wringing terror into red-shirt freshman and senior alike stared up blankly. There was nothing in those eyes now but a worn and defeated look, and it was a shock. So too the wrinkles in the shirt that was always pressed and pleated with military precision, the scuffed shoes and suddenly vulnerable-looking hands—even the Coach's brush cut, ordinarily as stiff and imperturbable as a falcon's crest, seemed to lie limp against his scalp. "Fontinot?" the Coach said finally, and his voice was dead.

"I, uh, just wanted to check—I mean, practice is at the regular time, right?"

Coach Tundra said nothing. He looked shrunken, lost, older in that moment than the oldest man in the oldest village in the mountains of Tibet. "There won't be any practice today," he said, rubbing his temple over the spot where the military surgeons had inserted the steel plate.

"No practice? But Coach, shouldn't we—I mean, don't we have to—"

"We can't field a team, Fontinot. I count sixteen guys out of forty-two that can go out there on the field and maybe come out of their comas for four consecutive quarters—and I'm counting you among them. And you're so banged up you can barely stand, let alone block." He heaved a sigh, plucked a torn battered shoe from the pile of relics on the floor and turned it over meditatively in his hands. "We're done, Fontinot. Finished. It's all she wrote. Like at Saigon when the gooks overran the place—it's time to cut our losses and run."

Ray Arthur Larry-Pete was stunned. He'd given his life for this, he'd sweated and fought and struggled, filled the bloated vessel of himself with the dregs of defeat, week after week, year after year. He was flunking all four of his Phys. Ed. courses, Suzie thought he was a clown, his mother was dying of uterine cancer, and his father—the man who'd named him after the three greatest offensive linemen in college-football history—was driving in from Cincinnati for the game, his last game, the ultimate and final contest that stood between him and the world of pay stubs and mortgages. "You don't mean," he stammered, "you don't mean we're going to *forfeit*, do you?"

For a long moment the Coach held him with his eyes. Faint sounds echoed in the corridors—the slap of sneakers, a door heaving closed, the far-off piping of the basketball coach's whistle. Coach Tundra made an unconscious gesture toward his pant leg and for a moment Ray Arthur Larry-Pete thought he was going to expose the prosthesis again. "What do you want me to do," he said finally, "go out there and play myself?"

Back in his room, Ray Arthur Larry-Pete brooded over the perfidy of it all. A few hours ago he'd been sick to death of the game—what had it gotten him but obloquy and bruises?—but now he wanted to go out there and play so badly he could kill for it. His roommate—Malmo Malmstein, the team's kicker—was still in the hospital, and he had the room to himself through the long morning and the interminable afternoon that followed it. He lay there prostrate on the bed like something shot out in the open that had crawled back to its cave to die, skipping classes, blowing off tests, and steeping himself in misery. At three he called Suzie—he had to talk to someone, anyone, or he'd go crazy—but one of her sorority sisters told him she was having her nails done and wasn't expected back before six. Her *nails*. Christ, that rubbed him raw: where was she when he needed her? A sick sinking feeling settled into his stomach—she was cutting him loose, he knew it.

And then, just as it was getting dark, at the very nadir of his despair, something snapped in him. What was wrong with him? Was he a quitter? A whiner and slacker? The kind of guy that gives up before he puts his cleats on? No way. Not Ray Arthur Larry-Pete Fontinot. He came up off the bed like some sort of volcanic eruption and lurched across the room to the phone. Sweating, ponderous, his very heart, lungs, and liver trembling with emotion, he focused all his concentration on the big pale block of his index finger as he dialed Gary Gedney, the chicken-neck who handled the equipment and kept the Gatorade bucket full. "Phone up all the guys," he roared into the receiver.

Gedney's voice came back at him in the thin whistling whine of a balloon sputtering round a room: "Who is this?"

"It's Fontinot. I want you to phone up all the guys."

"What for?" Gedney whined.

"We're calling a team meeting."

"Who is?"

Ray Arthur Larry-Pete considered the question a moment, and when finally he spoke it was with a conviction and authority he never thought he could command: "I am."

At seven that night, twenty-six members of the Caledonia Shuckers varsity football squad showed up in the lounge at Bloethal Hall. They filled the place with their presence, their sheer protoplasmic mass, and the chairs and couches groaned under the weight of them. They wore Band-Aids, gauze and tape—miles of it—and the lamplight caught the livid craters of their scars and glanced off the railway stitches running up and down their arms. There were casts, crutches, braces, slings. And there was the smell of them, a familiar, communal, lingering smell—the smell of a team.

Ray Arthur Larry-Pete Fontinot was ready for them, pacing back and forth in front of the sliding glass doors like a bear at the zoo, waiting patiently until each of them had gimped into the room and found a seat. Moss, DuBoy, and Kitwany were there with him for emotional support, as was the fifth interior lineman, center Brian McCornish. When they were all gathered, Ray Arthur Larry-Pete lifted his eyes and scanned the familiar faces of his teammates. "I don't know if any of you happened to notice," he said, "but here it is Monday night and we didn't have practice this afternoon."

"Amen," someone said, and a couple of the guys started hooting.

But Ray Arthur Larry-Pete Fontinot wasn't having any of it. He was a rock. His face hardened. He clenched his fists. "It's no joke," he bellowed, and the thunder of his voice set up sympathetic vibrations in the pole lamps with their stained and battered shades. "We've got five days to the biggest game of our lives, and I'm not just talking about us seniors, but everybody, and I want to know what we're going to do about it."

"Forfeit, that's what." It was Diderot, the third-string quarterback and the only one at that vital position who could stand without the aid of crutches. He was lounging against the wall in the back of the room, and all heads now turned to him. "I talked to Coach, and that's what he said."

In that moment, Ray Arthur Larry-Pete lost control of himself. "Forfeit, my ass!" he roared, slamming his forearm, cast and all, down on the nearest coffee table, which fell to splinters under the force of the blow. "Get up, guys," he hissed in an intense aside to his fellow linemen, and Moss, DuBoy, Kitwany, and McCornish rose beside him in a human wall. "We're willing to play sixty minutes of football," he boomed, and he had the attention of the room now, that was for sure. "Burt, Reggie, Steven, Brian, and me, and we'll play both ways, offense *and* defense, to fill in for guys with broken legs and concussions and whatnot—"

A murmur went up. This was crazy, insane, practically sacrificial. State gave out scholarships—and under-the-table payoffs too—and they got the really topflight players, the true behemoths and crackerjacks, the ones who attracted pro scouts and big money. To go up against them in their present condition would be like replaying the Gulf War, with Caledonia cast in the role of the Iraqis.

"What are you, a bunch of pussies?" Ray Arthur Larry-Pete cried. "Afraid to get your uniforms dirty? Afraid of a little contact? What do you want—to have to live with fifty-six-to-nothing for the rest of your life? Huh? I don't hear you!"

But they heard him. He pleaded, threatened, blustered, cajoled, took them aside one by one, jabbered into the phone half the night till his voice was hoarse and his ear felt like a piece of rubber grafted to the side of his head. In the end, they turned out for practice the following day—twenty-three of them, even Kitwany, who could barely move from the waist up and couldn't get a jersey on over his cast—and Ray Arthur Larry-Pete Fontinot ascended the three flights to the Coach's office and handed Coach Tundra the brand-new silver-plated whistle they'd chipped in to buy him. "Coach," he said, as the startled man looked up at him from the crucible of his memories, "we're ready to go out there and kick some butt."

The day of the game dawned cold and forbidding, with close skies, a biting wind and the threat of snow on the air. Ray Arthur Larry-Pete had lain awake half the night, his brain tumbling through all the permutations of victory and disaster like a slot machine gone amok. Would he shine? Would he rise to the occasion and fight off the devastating pass rush of State's gargantuan front four? And what about the defense? He hadn't played defense since junior high, and now, because they were shorthanded and because he'd opened his big mouth, he'd have to go both ways. Would he have the stamina? Or would he stagger round the field on rubber legs, thrust aside by State's steroid-swollen evolutionary freaks like the poor pathetic bumbling fat man he was destined to become? But no. Enough of that. If you thought like a loser—if you doubted for even a minute—then you were doomed, and you deserved 56–0 and worse.

At quarter to seven he got out of bed and stood in the center of the room in his undershorts, cutting the air savagely with the battering ram of his cast, pumping himself up. He felt unconquerable suddenly, felt blessed, felt as if he could do anything. The bruises, the swollen eye, the hip pointer, and rickety knees were nothing but fading memories now. By Tuesday he'd been able to lift both his arms to shoulder level without pain, and by Wednesday he was trotting round the field on a pair of legs that felt like bridge abutments. Thursday's scrimmage left him wanting more, and he flew like a sprinter through yesterday's light workout. He was as ready as he'd ever be.

At seven-fifteen he strode through the weather to the dining hall to load up on carbohydrates, and by eight he was standing like a colossus in the foyer of Suzie's sorority house. The whole campus had heard about his speech in the Bloethal lounge, and by Wednesday night Suzie had come back round again. They spent the night in his room—his private room, for the duration of Malmstein's stay at the Sisters of Mercy Hospital—and Suzie had traced his bruises with her lips and hugged the tractor tire of flesh he wore round his midsection to her own slim and naked self. Now she greeted him with wet hair and a face bereft of makeup. "Wish me luck, Suze," he said, and she clung to him briefly before going off to transform herself for the game.

Coach Tundra gathered his team in the locker room at twelve-thirty and spoke to them from his heart, employing the military conceits that always seemed to confuse the players as much as inspire them, and then they were thundering out onto the field like some crazed herd of hoofed and horned things with the scent of blood in their nostrils. The crowd roared. Caledonia's colors, chartreuse and orange, flew in the breeze. The band played. Warming up, Ray Arthur Larry-Pete could see Suzie sitting in the stands with her sorority sisters, her hair the color of vanilla ice cream, her mouth fallen open in a cry of savagery and bloodlust. And there, just to the rear of her—no, it couldn't be, it couldn't—but it was: his mom. Sitting there beside the hulking mass of his father, wrapped up in her windbreaker like a leaf pressed in an album, her scalp glinting bald through the dyed pouf of her hair, there she was, holding a feeble fist aloft. His *mom*! She'd been too sick to attend any of his games this year, but this was his last one, his last game ever, and she'd fought down her pain and all the unimaginable stress and suffering of the oncology ward just to see him play. He felt the tears come to his eyes as he raised his fist in harmony: this game was for her.

Unfortunately, within fifteen seconds of the kickoff, Caledonia was already in the hole, 7–0, and Ray Arthur Larry-Pete hadn't even got out onto the field yet. State's return man had fielded the kick at his own thirty after Malmstein's replacement, Hassan Farouk, had shanked the ball off the tee, and then he'd dodged past the entire special teams unit and on into the end zone as if the Caledonia players were molded of wax. On the ensuing kickoff, Bobby Bibby, a jittery, butterfingered guy Ray Arthur Larry-Pete had never liked, fumbled the ball, and State picked it up and ran it in for the score. They were less than a minute into the game, and already it was 14–0.

Ray Arthur Larry-Pete felt his heart sink, but he leapt up off the bench with a roar and butted heads so hard with Moss and DuBoy he almost knocked himself unconscious. "Come on, guys," he bellowed, "it's only fourteen points, it's nothing, bear down!" And then Bibby held on to the ball and Ray Arthur Larry-Pete was out on the field, going down in his three-point stance across from a guy who looked like a walking mountain. The guy had a handlebar mustache, little black eyes like hornets pinned to his head, and a long wicked annealed scar that plunged into his right eye socket and back out again. He looked to be about thirty, and he wore Number 95 stretched tight across the expanse of his chest. "You sorry sack of shit," he growled over Diderot's erratic snap-count. "I'm going to lay you flat out on your ass."

And that's exactly what he did. McCornish snapped the ball, Ray Arthur Larry-Pete felt something like a tactical nuclear explosion in the region of his sternum, and Number 95 was all over Diderot while Ray Arthur Larry-Pete stared up into the sky. In the next moment the trainer was out there, along with the Coach—already starting in on his Ia Drang Valley speech—and Ray Arthur Larry-Pete felt the first few snowflakes drift down into the whites of his wide-open and staring eyes. "Get up and walk it off," the trainer barked, and then half a dozen hands were pulling him to his feet, and Ray Arthur Larry-Pete Fontinot was back in his crouch, directly across from Number 95. And even then, though he hated to admit it to himself, though he was playing for Suzie and his mother and his own rapidly dissolving identity, he knew it was going to be a very long afternoon indeed.

It was 35–0 at the half, and Coach Tundra already had his pant leg rolled up by the time the team hobbled into the locker room. Frozen, pulverized, every cord, ligament, muscle, and fiber stretched to the breaking point, they listened numbly as the Coach went on about ordnance, landing zones, and fields of fire, while the trainer and his assistant scurried round plying tape, bandages, and the ever-present aerosol cans of Numzit. Kitwany's replacement, a huge amorphous red-faced freshman, sat in the corner, quietly weeping, and Bobby Bibby, who'd fumbled twice more in the second quarter, tore off his uniform, pulled on his street clothes without showering and walked on out the door. As for Ray Arthur Larry-Pete Fontinot, he lay supine on the cold hard tiles of the floor, every twinge, pull, ache, and contusion from the previous week's game reactivated, and a host of new ones cropping up to overload his nervous system. Along with Moss and DuBoy, he'd done double duty through the first thirty minutes—playing offense and defense both—and his legs were paralyzed. When the Coach blew his whistle and shouted, "On the attack, men!" Ray Arthur Larry-Pete had to be helped up off the floor.

The third quarter was a delirium of blowing snow, shouts, curses, and cries in the wilderness. Shadowy forms clashed and fell to the crunch of helmet and the clatter of shoulder pads. Ray Arthur Larry-Pete staggered around the field as if gutshot, so disoriented he was never quite certain which way his team was driving—or rather, being driven. But mercifully, the weather conditions slowed down the big blue barreling machine of State's offense, and by the time the gun sounded, they'd only been able to score once more.

And so the fourth quarter began, and while the stands emptied and even the most fanatical supporters sank glumly into their parkas, Caledonia limped out onto the field with their heads down and their jaws set in grim determination. They were no longer playing for pride, for the memories, for team spirit or their alma mater or to impress their girlfriends: they were playing for one thing only: to avoid at all cost the humiliation of 56–0. And they held on, grudging State every inch of the field, Ray Arthur Larry-Pete coming to life in sporadic flashes during which he was nearly lucid and more often than not moving in the right direction, Moss, DuBoy, and McCornish picking themselves up off the ground at regular intervals and the Coach hollering obscure instructions from the sidelines. With just under a minute left to play, they'd managed (with the help of what would turn out to be the worst blizzard to hit the area in twenty years) to hold State to only one touchdown more, making it 49–0 with the ball in their possession and the clock running down.

The snow blew in their teeth. State dug in. A feeble distant cheer went up from the invisible stands. And then, with Number 95 falling on him like an avalanche, Diderot fumbled, and State recovered. Two plays later, and with eight seconds left on the clock, they took the ball into the end zone to make it 55–0, and only the point-after attempt stood between Caledonia and the unforgivable, unutterable debasement of a second straight 56–0 drubbing. Ray Arthur Larry-Pete Fontinot extricated himself from the snowbank where Number 95 had left him and crept stiff-legged back to the line of scrimmage, where he would now assume the defensive role.

There was one hope, and one hope only, in that blasted naked dead cinder of a world that Ray Arthur Larry-Pete Fontinot and his hapless teammates unwillingly inhabited, and that was for one man among them to reach deep down inside himself and distill all his essence—all his wits, all his heart and the full power of his honed young musculature—into a single last-ditch attempt to block that kick. Ray Arthur Larry-Pete Fontinot looked into the frightened faces of his teammates as they heaved for breath in the defensive huddle and knew he was that man. "I'm going to block the kick," he said, and his voice sounded strange in his own ears. "I'm coming in from the right side and I'm going to block the kick." Moss's eyes were glazed. DuBoy was on the sidelines, vomiting in his helmet. No one said a word.

State lined up. Ray Arthur Larry-Pete took a deep breath. The ball was snapped, the lines crashed with a grunt and moan, and Ray Arthur Larry-Pete Fontinot launched himself at the kicker like the space shuttle coming in for a landing, and suddenly—miracle of miracles!—he felt the hard cold pellet of the ball glancing off the bandaged nubs of his fingers. A shout went up, and as he fell, as he slammed rib-first into the frozen ground, he watched the ball squirt up in the air and fall back into the arms of the kicker as if it were attached to a string, and then, unbelieving, he watched the kicker tuck the ball and sprint unmolested across the goal line for the two-point conversion.

If it weren't for Moss, they might never have found him. Ray Arthur Larry-Pete Fontinot just lay there where he'd fallen, the snow drifting silently round him, and he lay there long after the teams had left the field and the stands stood empty under a canopy of snow. There, in the dirt, the steady drift of snow gleaming against the exposed skin of his calves and slowly obliterating the number on the back of his jersey, he had a vision of the future. He saw himself working at some tedious, spirit-crushing job for which his Phys. Ed. training could never have prepared him, saw himself sunk in fat like his father, a pale plain wife and two grublike children at his side, no eighty-yard runs or blocked points to look back on through a false scrim of nostalgia, no glory and no defeat.

No defeat. It was a concept that seemed all at once to congeal in his tired brain, and as Moss called out his name and the snow beat down, he tried hard, with all his concentration, to hold it there.

(1992)

THE HIT MAN

Early Years

The Hit Man's early years are complicated by the black bag that he wears over his head. Teachers correct his pronunciation, the coach criticizes his attitude, the principal dresses him down for branding preschoolers with a lit cigarette. He is a poor student. At lunch he sits alone, feeding bell peppers and salami into the dark slot of his mouth. In the hallways, wiry young athletes snatch at the black hood and slap the back of his head. When he is thirteen he is approached by the captain of the football team, who pins him down and attempts to remove the hood. The Hit Man wastes him. Five years, says the judge.

Back on the Street

The Hit Man is back on the street in two months.

First Date

The girl's name is Cynthia. The Hit Man pulls up in front of her apartment in his father's hearse. (The Hit Man's father, whom he loathes and abominates, is a mortician. At breakfast the Hit Man's father had slapped the cornflakes from his son's bowl. The son threatened to waste his father. He did not, restrained no doubt by considerations of filial loyalty and the deep-seated taboos against patricide that permeate the universal unconscious.)

Cynthia's father has silver sideburns and plays tennis. He responds to the Hit Man's knock, expresses surprise at the Hit Man's appearance. The Hit Man takes Cynthia by the elbow, presses a twenty into her father's palm, and disappears into the night.

Father's Death

At breakfast the Hit Man slaps the cornflakes from his father's bowl. Then wastes him.

Mother's Death

The Hit Man is in his early twenties. He shoots pool, lifts weights, and drinks milk from the carton. His mother is in the hospital, dying of cancer or heart disease. The priest wears black. So does the Hit Man.

First Job

Porfirio Buñoz, a Cuban financier, invites the Hit Man to lunch. I hear you're looking for work, says Buñoz.

That's right, says the Hit Man.

Peas

The Hit Man does not like peas. They are too difficult to balance on the fork.

Talk Show

The Hit Man waits in the wings, the white slash of a cigarette scarring the midnight black of his head and upper torso. The makeup girl has done his mouth and eyes, brushed the nap of his hood. He has been briefed. The guest who precedes him is a pediatrician. A planetary glow washes the stage where the host and the pediatrician, separated by a potted palm, cross their legs and discuss the little disturbances of infants and toddlers.

After the station break the Hit Man finds himself squeezed into a director's chair, white lights in his eyes. The talk-show host is a baby-faced man in his early forties. He smiles like God and all His Angels. Well, he says. So you're a hit man. Tell me—I've always wanted to know—what does it feel like to hit someone?

Death of Mateo María Buñoz

The body of Mateo María Buñoz, the cousin and business associate of a prominent financier, is discovered down by the docks on a hot summer morning. Mist rises from the water like steam, there is the smell of fish. A large black bird perches on the dead man's forehead.

Marriage

Cynthia and the Hit Man stand at the altar, side by side. She is wearing a white satin gown and lace veil. The Hit Man has rented a tuxedo, extra-large, and a silk-lined black-velvet hood.

. . . Till death do you part, says the priest.

Moods

The Hit Man is moody, unpredictable. Once, in a luncheonette, the waitress brought him the meatloaf special but forgot to eliminate the peas. There was a spot of gravy on the Hit Man's hood, about where his chin should be. He looked up at the waitress, his eyes like pins behind the triangular slots, and wasted her.

Another time he went to the track with $25, came back with $1,800. He stopped at a cigar shop. As he stepped out of the shop a wino tugged at his sleeve and solicited a quarter. The Hit Man reached into his pocket, extracted the $1,800 and handed it to the wino. Then wasted him.

First Child

A boy. The Hit Man is delighted. He leans over the edge of the playpen and molds the tiny fingers around the grip of a nickel-plated derringer. The gun is loaded with blanks—the Hit Man wants the boy to get used to the noise. By the time he is four the boy has mastered the rudiments of Tae Kwon Do, can stick a knife in the wall from a distance of ten feet and shoot a moving target with either hand. The Hit Man rests his broad palm on the boy's head. You're going to make the Big Leagues, Tiger, he says.

Work

He flies to Cincinnati. To L.A. To Boston. To London. The stewardesses get to know him.

Half an Acre and a Garage

The Hit Man is raking leaves, amassing great brittle piles of them. He is wearing a black T-shirt, cut off at the shoulders, and a cotton work hood, also black. Cynthia is edging the flower bed, his son playing in the grass. The Hit Man waves to his neighbors as they drive by. The neighbors wave back.

When he has scoured the lawn to his satisfaction, the Hit Man draws the smaller leaf-hummocks together in a single mound the size of a pickup truck. Then he bends to ignite it with his lighter. Immediately, flames leap back from the leaves, cut channels through the pile, engulf it in a ball of fire. The Hit Man stands back, hands folded beneath the great meaty biceps. At his side is the three-headed dog. He bends to pat each of the heads, smoke and sparks raging against the sky.

Stalking the Streets of the City

He is stalking the streets of the city, collar up, brim down. It is late at night. He stalks past department stores, small businesses, parks, and gas stations. Past apartments, picket fences, picture windows. Dogs growl in the shadows, then slink away. He could hit any of us.

Retirement

A group of businessman-types—sixtyish, seventyish, portly, diamond rings, cigars, liver spots—throws him a party. Porfirio Buñoz, now in his eighties, makes a speech and presents the Hit Man with a gilded scythe. The Hit Man thanks him, then retires to the lake, where he can be seen in his speedboat, skating out over the blue, hood rippling in the breeze.

Death

He is stricken, shrunken, half his former self. He lies propped against the pillows at Mercy Hospital, a bank of gentians drooping round the bed. Tubes run into the hood at the nostril openings, his eyes are clouded and red, sunk deep behind the triangular slots. The priest wears black. So does the Hit Man.

On the other side of town the Hit Man's son is standing before the mirror of a shop that specializes in Hit Man attire. Trying on his first hood.

(1977)

ALMOST SHOOTING AN ELEPHANT

So we went in there with Meghalaya Cable, a subsidiary of Verizon (don't ask, because I couldn't begin to tell you: just think multinational, that's all), and put in the grid so these people could have color TV and DSL hookups in their huts, and I brought a couple rifles with me. I like to hunt, all right? So crucify me. I grew up in Iowa, in Ottumwa, and it was a rare day when I didn't bring something home for my mother, whether it was ringneck or rabbit or even a gopher or muskrat, which are not bad eating if you stew them up with tomatoes and onions, and plus you get your fur. I had to pay an excess baggage charge, which the company declined to pick up, but there was no way I was going to India without my guns. Especially since this leg of the project was in the West Garo Hills, where they still have the kind of jungle they had in Kipling's day. Or at least remnants of it.

Anyway, it was my day off and I was lying up in my tent, slapping mosquitoes and leafing through a back issue of *Guns & Ammo*, the birds screeching in the trees, the heat delivering one knockout punch after another till I could barely hold my head up. I wouldn't say I was bored—I was putting in a six-day workweek stringing wire to one ramshackle village after another, and just to lie there and feel the cot give under my bones was a luxury. Still, it felt as if the hands of my watch hadn't moved in the last hour and as I drifted in and out of sleep the birds always seemed to be hitting the same note. I tried to relax, enjoy the moment and the magazine, but I was only waiting for the heat to let up so I could take my .22 and a jar of the local rice beer down the hill to the swamp and see what was stirring in the bushes.

I was studying the ads in the back of the magazine—a party in Wishbone, Montana, was offering a classic Mannlicher-Schoenauer carbine with a Monte Carlo stock for sale or trade, a weapon I would have killed for—when I heard the sound of footsteps approaching on the path up from the village. Flip-flops. You could hear them a mile away, a slap, a shuffle, another slap, and then a quick burst: *slap, slap, slap*. There was a pause and I felt the bamboo platform rock ever so slightly.

The birds stopped screeching, all at once, as if the point of contention, whatever it was, had slipped their bird brains. A smell of meat roasting over the open fire came wafting up the hill on the first hint of an evening breeze. In the sudden hush I heard the frogs belching in the ditch behind me and the faintest thumping strains of Lynyrd Skynyrd's "Free Bird" from a radio in one of the other tents. "Randall? You in there?" came a voice just outside the front flap.

This was a female voice, and my hope (notwithstanding the fact that I was, and am, totally attached to Jenny, who I'm saving to buy a condo with in Des Moines) was that it was Poonam. Poonam was from Bombay, she wore tight jeans and little knit blouses that left her midriff bare, and she was doing her PhD thesis on the Garos and their religious beliefs. She'd been waiting for me with a bottle of gin and a plate of curry when I got off work two days earlier, and I have to admit that the sound of her voice—she spoke very softly, so you had to strain to hear—put me in a sort of trance that wouldn't seem to let up, and I'd begun to entertain thoughts about what she might look like without the jeans and blouse. All she could talk about was her research, of course, and that was fine by me, because with the gin and the curry and the sweet, soft music of her voice she could have been lecturing on the Bombay sewer system and I would have been rooted to the spot. (And what *did* the Garos believe in? Well, they called themselves Christians—they'd been converted under the British Raj—but in actuality they were animists, absolutely dead certain that spirits inhabited the trees, the earth, the creatures of the forest, and that those spirits were just about universally evil. That is, life was shit—rats in the granaries, elephants obliterating the fields, kraits and cobras killing the children the leopards hadn't made off with, floods and droughts and diseases that didn't even have names— and whoever was responsible for it had to be as malicious as a whole squad of devils.)

So I said, "Yeah, I'm here," expecting Poonam, expecting gin, religion, and a sweet little roll of belly flesh I could almost taste with the tip of a stiff tongue going south, and who should part the flaps but Candi Berkee, my coworker from New Jersey whose presence there, in my tent in the West Garo Hills, was a real testimony to Verizon's commitment to equal-opportunity employment.

"Hi," she said.

"'S up?" I said.

She gave a sort of full-body shrug, her lips crushed together under the weight of her nose and the *Matrix*-style shades that never left her face, then ducked through the flaps and flopped down in my camp chair. Which was piled high with six or seven sedimentary layers of used socks, underwear, and T-shirts I refrained from tossing on the floor for fear of what might end up living inside them. "I don't know," she said, dropping her face as if she were emptying a pan of dishwater, "I'm just bored. This is a boring place. The most boring place in the world. Number one. Know what I mean?"

It wasn't that she was unattractive—bodywise, she was off the charts—but there was something about her that irritated me, and it went beyond her unrelenting whining about the heat, the mosquitoes, the food, the tedium, and anything else she could think of. For one thing, she was a militant vegetarian who regarded anyone who even thought of hunting as the lowest of the low, a step below the average Al Quaeda terrorist ("At least they *believe* in something"). For another, her taste in music—Britney, Whitney, and Mariah—was as pathetic as you could get. The fact that she was in my tent was a strong indicator that everybody else must have gone into Tura, the nearest excuse for a city. Either that or committed suicide.

I didn't respond. The cot cupped my bones. She was wearing shorts and a bikini top, and there was a bright sheen of sweat on her exposed flesh that made her look as if she'd been greased for the flagpole event at the county fair. The birds started in again: *screech*, *screech*, *screech*.

"You want to smoke out?"

She knew I had pot. I knew she had pot. Everybody had pot. The whole country was made out of it. I was about to beg off on the grounds that I had to keep my senses sharp for putting bullets into whatever might be creeping down to the river to sneak a drink, be it muntjac or macaque, but thought better of it—I was in no mood for a lecture. "Nah," I said finally, sucking all the enthusiasm out of my voice. "I don't think so. Not today."

"Why not?" She shoved her sweat-limp hair out of her eyes and gave me an accusatory look. "Come on, don't be a pussy. Help me out here. I'm bored. Did I tell you that? Bored with a capital *B*."

I don't know whether the birds cut off before or after the sound of a second pair of flip-flops came to me, but there it was—the slap, the shuffle, and then the give of the bamboo floor. "Hello?" Poonam's voice. "Hello, Randall?"

Poonam wasn't exactly overjoyed to see Candi there, and for her part, Candi wasn't too thrilled either. I'd been up front with both of them about Jenny, but when you're away from home and affection long enough, strange things begin to happen, and I suppose hunting can only take you so far. As a distraction, that is.

"Oh . . . hi," Poonam murmured, shifting her eyes from me to

Candi and back again. "I was just—" She looked down at the floor. "I was just coming for Randall, because the Wangala celebration is about to begin, or the drumming anyway—we won't see the dancing till tomorrow, officially—and I wondered if, well" (up came the eyes, full and bright, like high beams on a dark country road), "if you wanted to come with me to the village and see what they're doing— the ritual, I mean. Because it's, well, I find it stimulating. And I think you would too, Randall." She turned to Candi then, because Poonam was graceful and pretty and she had manners to spare. "And you too, Candi. You're welcome too."

I'm no expert, but from what Poonam told me, the Garos have a number of celebrations during the year, no different from the puffed-up Christians of Ottumwa and environs, and this one— Wangala—was a harvest festival. Think Thanksgiving, but a whole lot more primitive. Or maybe "rootsier" is a better word. Who are *we* thanking? God, supposedly, but in Ottumwa, it's more like Wal-Mart or Hy-Vee. The Garos, on the other hand, are doing obeisance to Saljong, god of fertility, who provides nature's bounty in the forms of crops and fish and game. Of course, Poonam never did tell me what they expected to happen if they didn't give their abundant thanks to this particular god, but I could guess.

Anyway, the three of us went down the hill to the village amid the bird-screech and the smell of dung and cook-fires, and Candi fired up a bowl and passed it round and Poonam and I took our turns, because I figured, why not? The muntjacs could wait till tomorrow, and this, whatever it might turn out to be, was something different at least, not to mention the fact that Poonam was there at my side with her slim, smooth limbs and the revelation of flesh that defined her hipbones and navel. "Do you feel anything?" Candi kept saying. "You want to do another hit? Randall? Poonam?" Half a dozen chickens fanned out across the path and vanished in the undergrowth. The sun inflamed the trees.

In the village itself—foot-tamped dirt, cane and thatch huts on raised platforms of bamboo, lurking rack-ribbed dogs, more bird-screech—people were preparing the evening meal in their courtyards. The smoke was fragrant with curry and vindaloo, triggering my salivary glands to clench and clench again. A pig gave us a malicious look from beneath one of the huts and I couldn't help laughing—the thing wouldn't have even come up to the hocks of one of our Iowa hogs. "What are you talking, *drums*?" Candi said. "I don't hear any drums."

Overhead, the high-voltage wires bellied between the electric poles, at least half of which we'd had to replace with the new high-resin-compound model that resists rot and termite damage, and you wouldn't believe what the climate here can do to a piece of creosote-soaked wood stuck in the ground—but don't get me started. Just looking at the things made my back ache. Poonam was about to say something in response, something cutting or at least impatient—I could tell from the way she bit her underlip—when all at once the drums started up from the rear of the village, where the bachelors had their quarters. There was a hollow booming and then a deeper thump that seemed to ignite a furious, palm-driven rhythm pulsing beneath it. Children began to sprint past us.

Instantly I was caught up in the excitement. I felt like a kid at the start of the Memorial Day parade, with the high-school band warming up the snare drums, the horses beating at the pavement in impatience, and the mayor goosing his white Cadillac convertible with the beauty queen arrayed in back. I'd heard some of the local music before—my best bud in the village, Dakgipa, played a thing like an oversized recorder, and he could really do on it too, knocking out the melodies to "Smells Like Teen Spirit" and "Paranoid Android" as if he'd written them himself—but it was nothing like the ferment of those drums. I glanced at Poonam and she gave me a smile so muscular it showed all her bright, perfect teeth and lifted her right nostril so that her nose ring caught the light and winked at me. "All right," I said. "Party time!"

And that was how it went. Everybody knew us—the Garos are not in the least bit standoffish or uptight or whatever you want to call it—and before long we were sitting cross-legged in the court-yard with plates of food in our laps and jars of rice beer in hand while the bachelors went at it on every sort of drum imaginable—the *Ambengdama*, the *Chisakdama*, *Atong dama*, *Ruga* and *Chibok dama*, the *Nagra* and *Kram*. And gongs. They were big on gongs too. Candi wouldn't touch the food—she'd been down with one stomach ailment after another, right from orientation on—but she drained that beer as if she were at a kegger on Long Beach Island, while Poonam sat beside me on a clump of grass with her flawless posture and sweet, compressed smile.

At one point—my recollection isn't too clear here, I'm afraid, after the weed and the beer, not to mention the flamingest curry I've ever yet to this day run across—Dakgipa came and sat with us and we made a date to go hunting the following day after work. Dakgipa spent all his free time out in the bush, snaring squirrels, bandicoots, and the black-napped hare and the like, potting green pigeons in the trees and crow pheasants out in the fields, and he'd acted as a sort of guide for me, teaching me the habits of the local game and helping me tan the hides to ship back home so Jenny and I could stretch them decoratively over the walls of our condo-to-be. There was a quid pro quo, of course—Dak was a Counter-Strike addict and all he could talk about was the DSL capability he fervently hoped we were bringing him and the 10Base-T Ethernet network interface cards he expected we'd hand out to go with the new modems we were seeding the village with. But that was okay. That was cool. He gave me the binturong and the masked palm civet and I gave him the promise of high-speed Internet.

It grew dark. The mosquitoes settled in for their own feast, and even as the screeching day birds flew off to their roosts the night creatures took up the complaint, which sizzled through the quieter moments of the drummers' repertoire like some sort of weird natural distortion, as if the gods of the jungle had their amps cranked too high. I was aware of Poonam beside me, Dak was sounding out Candi on the perennial question of Mac versus PC, and the drums had sunk down to the hypnotic pulse of water flowing in its eternal cycle—everything gone calm and mellow. After a long silence, Poonam turned to me. "Did you know the auntie of my host family was carried off by a *bhut* the other night?"

I didn't know. Hadn't heard. Poonam's skin glowed in the light of the bonfire somebody had lit while I was dreaming the same dream as the drummers, and her eyes opened up to me so that I wanted to crawl inside them and forever forget Jenny and Des Moines and the Appleseed Condo Corp. Inc. "What's a *bhut*?" I asked.

"A forest spirit."

"A what? Don't tell me you actually—?" I caught myself and never finished the thought. I didn't want to sound too harsh because we were just starting to have a real meeting of the minds and a meeting of the minds is—or can be, or ought to be—a prelude to a meeting of the flesh.

Her smile was softer, more serene than ever. "It was in the form of a leopard," she said. "*Bhuts* often take on the shape of that sneaking thief of the night. They come for adulterers, Randall, false-promisers, moneylenders, for the loose and easy. Some nights, they just take what they can get."

I stared off into the fire, at the shapes that shifted there like souls come to life. "And the auntie—what did she do?"

Poonam gave an elaborate shrug. "They say she ate the flesh of the forest creatures without making sacrifice. But you'd have to believe, wouldn't you, to put any credence in a primitive speculation like that?" The drums flowed, things crept unseen through the high grass. "Just think of it, Randall," she said, rotating her hips so that she was facing me square on, "all these people through all these eons and when they go out to make water at night they might never come back, grandmother vanished on her way to the well, your childhood dog disappeared like smoke, your own children carried off. And you ask me if I *believe*?"

Maybe it was the pot, maybe that was it, but suddenly I felt uneasy, as if the whole world were holding its breath and watching me and me alone. "But you said it yourself—it's only a leopard."

"Only?"

I didn't know what to say to this. The fact was I'd never shot anything larger than a six-point buck on the edge of a soybean field; the biggest predators we had in Iowa were fox, bobcat, and coyote, nothing that could creep up on you without a sound and crush your skull in its jaws while simultaneously raking out your intestines with swift, knifing thrusts of its hind claws. That was a big "only."

"Would you hunt such a thing, Randall? In the night? Would you?"

Candi was deep in conversation with Dak when Poonam and I excused ourselves to stroll back up the hill to my tent ("Yes," Dak was saying, "but what sort of throughput speed can you offer?"). I'd felt so mellow and so—detached, I'd guess you'd call it, from Jenny that I found myself leaning into Poonam and putting my lips to her ear just as the drummers leapfrogged up the scale of intensity and the ground and the thatch and even the leaves of the bushes began to vibrate. It was hot. I was sweating from every pore. There was nothing in the world but drums. Drums were my essence, drums were the rain and the sunshine after a storm, they were the beginning and the end, the stars, the deeps—but I don't want to get too carried away here. You get the idea: my lips, Poonam's ear. "Would you—" I began, and I had to shout to hear myself, "I mean, would you want to come back to the tent for a nightcap maybe? With me?"

She smelled of palm oil—or maybe it was Nivea. She was shy, and so was I. "Yes," she whispered, the sound all but lost in the tumult around us. But then she shrugged for emphasis and added, "Sure, why not?"

The night sustained us, the hill melted away. Her hand found mine in the dark. For a long while we sat side by side on my cot, mixing fresh-squeezed lime juice, confectioners' sugar, and Tanqueray in my only glass and taking turns watching each other drink from it, and then she subsided against me, against my chest and the circulatory organ that was pounding away there—my heart, that is—and eventually I got to see what she looked like without the little knit blouse and the tight jeans and I fell away to the pulse of the drums and the image of a swift, spotted *bhut* stalking the night.

I woke with a jolt. It was dark still, the drums silent, the birds and monkeys nodding on their hidden perches, the chirring of the insects fading into the background like white noise. Somewhere, deep in my dream, someone had been screaming—and this was no ordinary scream, no mere wringing out of fear or excitement, but something darker, deeper, more hurtful and wicked—and now, awake, I heard it again. Poonam sat up beside me. "Jesus," I said. "What was that?"

She didn't say I told you so, didn't say it was a leopard or a *bhut* or the creeping manifestation of the Christian Devil himself, because there was no time for that or anything else: the platform swayed under the weight of an animate being and I never thought to reach for my rifle or even my boxers. For an interminable time I sat there rigid in the dark, Poonam's nails digging into my shoulder, neither of us breathing—*Jenny*, I was thinking, *Jenny*—until the flaps parted on the gray seep of dawn and Dak thrust his agitated face into the tent. "Randall," he barked. "Randall—oh, shit! Shit! Have you got your gun, your rifle? Get your rifle. Bring it! Quick!" I could hear the birds now—first one started in and then they were all instantaneously competing to screech it down—and Poonam loosened her grip on my arm.

"What is it? What's the problem?" I couldn't really hear myself, but I have no doubt my voice was unsteady, because on some level—scratch that: on every level—I didn't want to know and certainly didn't want to have to go off into the bush after whatever it was that had made that unholy rupture in the fabric of the night.

Dak's face just hung there, astonished, a caricature of impatience and exasperation, though I couldn't see his eyes (for some reason—and this struck me as maybe the oddest thing about the whole situation—he was wearing Candi's *Matrix* shades). "The big one," he said. "The biggest bore you have."

"For what? Why? What's the deal?" Though our entire exchange could have been compacted into the space of maybe ten seconds, I was stalling, no doubt about it.

His response, delivered through clenched teeth, completely threw me. I don't know what I'd expected—demons, man-eaters, Bangladeshi terrorists—but probably the last thing was elephants. "Elephants?" I repeated stupidly. To tell you the truth, I'd pretty much forgotten they even had elephants out there in the bush—sure, people still used them to haul things, like telephone poles, for instance, but those elephants were as tame as lapdogs and no more noticeable or threatening than a big gray stucco wall.

I still hadn't moved. Poonam shielded herself from Dak—as if, in this moment of fomenting crisis, he would have been interested in the shape of her breasts—and before I'd even reached for my shorts she had the knit blouse over her head and was smoothing it down under her rib cage.

What had happened, apparently, was that the wild elephants had come thundering out of the jungle at first light to ravage the village and raid the crops. All I could think of were those old Tarzan movies—I mean, really: *elephants*? "You're joking, right, Dak?" I said, reaching for my clothes. "It's like the April Fool's, right—part of the whole Wangala thing? Tell me you're joking."

I'd never heard Dak raise his voice before—he was so together, so calm and focused, he was almost holy—but he raised it now. "Will you fucking wake up to what I'm telling you, Randall—they're wrecking the place, going for the granary, trampling the fields. Worse—they're drunk!"

"Drunk?"

His face collapsed, his shoulders sank. "They got the rice beer. All of it."

And so, that was how I found myself stalking the streets of the village ten minutes later, the very sweaty stock of a very inadequate rifle in my hand. The place was unrecognizable. Trees had been uprooted, the huts crushed, the carcasses of pigs, chickens, and goats scattered like trash. Smoke rose from the ruins where early-morning cook-fires had gone out of control and begun to swallow up the splinters of the huts, even as people ran around frantically with leaking buckets of water. There was one man dead in the street and I'd never seen a dead human being before, both sets of my grandparents having opted for cremation to spare us the mortuary and the open casket and the waxen effigies propped within. He was lying on his face in the dirt, the skin stripped from his back like the husk of a banana, his head radically compressed. I couldn't be sure, but I thought I recognized him as one of the drummers from the previous night. I felt something rise in my throat, a lump of it burning there.

That was when the villagers caught sight of me, caught sight of the rifle. Within minutes I'd attracted a vengeful, hysterical crowd, everybody jabbering and gesticulating and singing their own little song of woe, and me at the head of the mob, utterly clueless. The rifle in my hands—a 7mm Remington—was no elephant gun. Far from it. It packed some stopping power, sure, and I'd brought it along in the unlikely event I could get a shot at something big, a gaur or maybe even a leopard or (crucify me) a tiger. Back in Ottumwa I suppose I'd entertained a fantasy about coming down some sun-spangled path and seeing a big flat-headed Bengal tiger making off with somebody's dog and dropping him with a single, perfect heart shot and then paying a bunch of worshipful coolies or natives or whoever they might be to skin it out so Jenny and I could hang it on the wall and I could have a story to tell over the course of the next thousand backyard barbecues. But that was the fantasy and this was the reality. To stop an elephant—even to put a scare into one—you needed a lot more firepower than I had. And experience—experience wouldn't hurt either.

The noise level—people squabbling and shouting, the eternal birds, dogs howling—was getting to me. How could anybody expect me to stalk an animal with this circus at my back? I looked around for Dak, hoping he could do something to distract the mob so that I could have some peace to prop myself up and stop the heaviness in my legs from climbing up over my belt and paralyzing me. I'd never been more afraid in my life, and I didn't know what was worse— having to shoot something the size of a house without getting trampled or looking like a fool, coward, and wimp in the face of all these people. Like it or not, I was the one with the gun, the white man, the pukka sahib; I was the torchbearer of Western superiority, the one with everything to prove and everything to lose. How had I gotten myself into this? Just because I liked to hunt? Because I'd potted a bandicoot or two and the entire village knew it? And this wasn't just one elephant, which would have been bad enough, but a whole herd—and they were drunk, and who knew what that would do to their judgment?

The crowd pushed me forward like the surge of the tide and I looked in vain for Dak—for a friendly face, for anybody—until finally I spotted him at the rear of the press, with Candi and Poonam at his side, all three of them looking as if they'd just vomited up breakfast. I gave them a sick wave—there was nothing else I could do—and came round a corner to see two other corpses laid out in the street as if they were sleeping on very thin mattresses. And then, suddenly, the crowd fell silent.

There before me was an elephant. Or the truck-high back end of one. It was standing in the shell of a hut, its head bent forward as it sucked rice beer up its trunk from an open cask that somehow, crazily, had remained upright through all the preceding chaos. I remember thinking what an amazing animal this was—a kind of animate bull-dozer, and it lived right out there in the jungle, invisible to everybody but the birds, as stealthy as a rat—and wondered what we'd do if we had things like this back home, ready to burst out of the river bottom and lay waste to the cornfields on their way to Kenny's Bar and Grill to tap half a dozen kegs at a time. The thought was short-lived. Because the thing had lifted its head and craned its neck—if it even had a neck—to look back over its shoulder and fan its ears, which were like big tattered flags of flesh. Reflexively I looked over my shoulder and discovered that I was alone—the villagers had cleared off to a distance of five hundred feet, as if the tide had suddenly receded. How did I feel about that? For one thing, it made my legs go even heavier—they were pillars, they were made of concrete, marble, lead, and I couldn't have run if I'd wanted to. For another, I began a grisly calculation—as long as the crowd had been with me, the elephant would have had a degree of choice as to just who it wanted to obliterate. Now that choice had been drastically reduced.

Very slowly—infinitely slowly, millimeter by millimeter—I began to move to my right, the rifle at my shoulder, the cartridge in the chamber, my finger frozen at the trigger. I needed to get broad-side of the thing, which had gone back to drinking beer now, pausing to snort or to tear up a patch of long grass and beat it against its knees in a nice calm undrunken grandmotherly kind of way that lulled me for an instant. But really, I didn't have a clue. I remem-bered the Orwell essay, which *Guns & Ammo* reprinted every couple of years by way of thrilling the reading public with the fantasy of bringing down the ultimate trophy animal, and how Orwell said he'd thought the thing's brain was just back of the eyes. My right arm felt as if it was in a cast. My trigger finger swelled up to the size of a base-ball bat. I couldn't seem to breathe.

That was when the elephant gave a sudden lurch and swung around amid the shattered bamboo and the tatters of thatch to face me head-on. Boom: it happened in an instant. There the thing was, fifty feet away—four quick elephantine strides—stinking and titanic, staggering from one foot to the other like one of the street people you see on the sidewalks of San Francisco or New York. It seemed perplexed, as if it couldn't remember what it was doing there with all that wreckage scattered around it—and I had to credit the beer for that. Those fermenting tubs hold something like fifty gallons each, and that's a lot of beer by anybody's standards, even an elephant's. The smallest ray of hope stirred in me—maybe, if I just stood rock still, the thing wouldn't see me. Or couldn't. Maybe it would just stagger into the jungle to sleep it off and I could save face by blowing a couple shots over its retreating butt.

But that wasn't what happened.

The unreadable red-rimmed eyes seemed to seize on me and the thing threw back its head with one of those maniacal trumpeting blasts we all recognize, anybody who's got a TV, anyway, and then, quite plainly berserk, it came for me. I'd like to say I stood my ground, calmly pumping off round after round until the thing dropped massively at my feet, but that didn't happen either. All at once my legs felt light again, as if they weren't legs at all but things shaped out of air, and I dropped the gun and ran like I'd never run before in my life. And the crowd—all those irate Garo tribesmen, Dak and Candi and Poonam and whoever else was crazy enough to be out there watching this little slice of drama—they turned and ran too, but of course they had a good head start on me, and even if I'd just come off a first-place finish in the hundred meters at the Olympics, the elephant would have caught up to me in a heartbeat and transformed me into a section of roadway and all the money my parents had laid out on orthodontics and tuition and just plain food would have been for naught. I hadn't gone ten paces before an errant fragment of thatch roof caught hold of my foot and down I went, expecting imminent transformation (or pancakeization, as Poonam later phrased it, and I didn't think it was that funny, believe me).

The elephant had been trumpeting madly but suddenly the high notes shot right off the scale and I lifted my fragile head to see what I at first thought was some sort of giant black snake cavorting with the thing. I'll tell you, the elephant was lively now, dancing right up off its toes as if it wanted to fly away. It took a moment to come together for me: that was no snake—that was the high-voltage cable and that thing at the other end of it was the snapped-off, bobbing remnant of a high-resin-compound utility pole. The dance was energetic, almost high-spirited, but it was over in an instant, and when the thing came down—the elephant, big as an eighteen-wheeler—the ground shook as if a whole city had collapsed.

There was dust everywhere. The cable whipped and sparked. I heard the crowd roar and reverse itself, a hundred feet pounding at the dirt, and then, in the midst of it all, there was that scream again, the one I'd heard in the night; it was like someone slipping a knife up under my rib cage and twisting it. My gaze leapt past the hulk of the elephant, past the ruin of the village and the pall of smoke, to the shadowy architecture of the jungle. And there it was, the spotted thing, crouching on all fours with its eyes fastened on me, raging yellow, raging, until it rose on two legs and vanished.

(2004)

JULIANA CLOTH

She was just sixteen, and still under her mother's wing, when William Wamala first came to town with his bright bolts of cloth. He was a trader from the North, and he'd come across the vast gray plane of the lake so early in the morning he was like a ghost rising from the mist. Picture him there, out on the lake, the cylinders of rich cotton batik hanging limp over the prow of the invisible boat as if suspended in ether, no movement discernible but for the distant dip and rise of his arms, and all the birds crying out, startled, while the naked statue of his torso levitated above the still and glassy surface. The fishermen were the first to see him coming. They were the eyes of the village, just as the dogs were its nose, and as they cast their nets for *dagaa* they raised their palms in silent greeting.

Miriam—she was the only child of Ann Namirimu and the late Joseph Namirimu, who had been struck by lightning and scorched out of this existence when she was an infant strapped to her mother's back—was at first unaware that the trader had arrived in town with a new season's patterns. She was asleep at such an hour, crushed under the weight of her sixteen years and the disco dance she'd attended the night before with her aunt Abusaga and uncle Milton Metembe. Uncle Milton's special friend, Gladys Makuma, had been there, and he danced with her all night while Aunt Abusaga danced with Miriam and a mural of boys and men painted themselves to the walls, alive only in their eyes. People were smoking and drinking beer and whiskey. The music thumped with a percussive bass, and the beat held steady except in those intervals when the electricity faltered and people fell laughing into each other's arms. It was like Heaven, a picture-book Heaven, and Miriam, asleep, lived only to go back there and dance till her feet got so heavy she couldn't lift them.

Coffee woke her. And griddle cakes. And the crowing of fugitive cocks. Her mother, richly draped in last year's *kanga* and exuding a smell of warm sheets and butter, was fixing breakfast preparatory to her departure to the government office where she worked as a secretary. Miriam got up, and her dog got up with her. She ate with her mother in silence, sitting at the polished wooden table as if she were chained to it.

When her mother had left for work, Miriam dug a pack of cigarettes from an innocent-looking fold of her bedclothes and stuck one experimentally in the corner of her mouth. They were Top Club cigarettes ("For Men Whose Decisions Are Final") and they'd been slipped into her hand at the disco dance, right there in the middle of the floor, while she was rolling her hips and cranking her shoulders in sync with the beat. And who had slipped them to her, unlooked for and unasked for, as a kind of tribute? A boy she'd known all her life, James Kariango, who was eighteen years old and as tall and wide-shouldered as any man. She felt a hand touch hers as everyone moved in a blur of limbs through sweat that was like a wall, the fumes of whiskey rose from the makeshift bar, and the shadowy blue clouds of smoke hung like curtains around imaginary windows, and there he was, dancing with a woman she'd never seen before and eclipsing his left eye in a sly wink.

She had never smoked a cigarette. Her mother wouldn't allow it. Cigarettes were for common people, and Ann Namirimu was no common person—educated in the capital and sister to one of the president's top advisers—and neither was her daughter. Her daughter was a lady, one of only eight girls in the village to go on to high school, and she would conduct herself like a lady at all times or suffer the rolling thunder and sudden strikes of her mother's wrath, and, while Aunt Abusaga and Uncle Milton Metembe might have thought a disco dance appropriate for a young lady, Ann Namirimu certainly did not, and it was against her better judgment that Miriam had been allowed to go at all. Still, once Miriam had stuck the cigarette in her mouth and studied herself in the mirror from various angles, she couldn't help putting a match to the tip of it and letting the sweet stinging smoke invade her mouth and swell out her cheeks until she exhaled like a veteran. She never took the smoke into her lungs, and she didn't really like the taste of it, but she smoked the cigarette down to a nub, watching herself in the mirror all the while, and then she went out into the yard and carefully buried the remnant where her mother wouldn't find it.

She fed her dog, swept the mats, and dressed for school in a dream oriented around the pulse of disco music and the movement of liberated bodies. Then she went off to school, barefoot, carrying her shoes in one hand and her satchel of books and papers in the other, thinking she might just have a peek at the market on her way.

It was early still, the sun long in the trees and all the striped and spotted dogs of the town stretching and yawning in the street, but it might as well have been noon in the marketplace. Everyone was there. Farmwives with their yams and tomatoes arranged in baskets and laid out on straw mats, a man selling smoked colobus monkey and *pangas* honed to a killing edge, the fishermen with their fresh-caught tilapia and tiger fish, the game and cattle butchers and the convocation of flies that had gathered to taste the wet sweetness of the carcasses dangling from metal hooks. And the crafts merchants, too—the women selling bright orange and yellow plastic bowls, pottery, mats and rugs and cloth. Cloth especially. And that was where Miriam found him, William Wamala, the smiling, handsome, persuasive young man and budding entrepreneur from the North, and his fine print cotton cloth, his Juliana cloth.

For that was what they christened it that morning, the crowd gathered around his stall that was nothing more than a rickety table set up at the far end of the marketplace where no one bothered about anything: Juliana cloth. William Wamala stood behind the table with his measuring tape and shears and the bolts of cloth in a blue so deep you fell into it, with slashes of pale papaya and bright arterial red for contrast. "How much for the Juliana cloth?" one woman asked, and they all knew the name was right as soon as she'd pronounced it. Because this print, unlike any they'd seen before, didn't feature flowers or birds or palm fronds or the geometric patterns that had become so popular in the last few years but a name—a name in English, a big, bold name spelled out in the aforementioned colors that ran in crazy zigzags all over the deep-blue field. "Juliana," it read. "Juliana, Juliana, Juliana."

Miriam wanted the cloth as soon as she saw it. Everyone wanted it. Everyone wanted to be the first to appear in the streets or at the disco dance in a *kanga* cut from this scintillating and enticing cloth. But it was expensive. Very expensive. And exclusive to William Wamala. Who proved ultimately to be a very understanding and affectionate young man, willing to barter and trade if shillings were unavailable, accepting pots of honey, dried *dagaa*, beer, whiskey, and cigarettes in payment, and especially, when it came to the beauties of the town, exchanging his Juliana cloth for what might be considered their most precious commodity, a commodity that cost them nothing but pleasure in the trading.

When Miriam stopped in the market two mornings later, he was there still, but the crowd around him was smaller and the bolts of cloth much depleted. He sat back now in a new cane chair, his splayed feet crossed at the ankles and looming large over the scrap-strewn table, his smile a bit haggard, a beer pressed like a jewel to his lips. "Hello, Little Miss," he crooned in a booming basso when he saw her standing there with her satchel between two fat-armed women wrapped in *kangas* that were as ancient as dust and not much prettier.

She looked him in the eye. There was nothing to be afraid of: Beryl Obote, fifteen and resplendent in Juliana cloth, had told her all about him, how he hummed and sang while removing a girl's clothes and how insatiable he was, as if that very day were his last on earth. "Hello," Miriam said, smiling widely. "I was just wondering how much the Juliana cloth is today?"

"For you?" He never even bothered to remove his feet from the table, and she could see the faintest glimmer of interest rising from the deeps of his eyes like a lonely fish, only to sink back down again into the murk. He was satiated, bloated with drink and drugs and rich food, rubbed so raw between his legs he could scarcely walk, and she was no beauty, she knew that. She made her eyes big. She held her breath. Finally, while the fat-armed women bickered over something in thin piping voices and the sun vaulted through the trees to take hold of her face, he quoted her a price. In shillings.

The first to fall ill was Gladys Makuma, Uncle Milton Metembe's special friend. It was during the long rains in April, and many people were sick with one thing or another, and no one thought much about it at first. "Let her rest," Miriam's mother insisted from her long slab of an aristocrat's face. "Give her tea with lemon and honey and an herbal broth in the evenings, and she'll soon be on her feet again." But Miriam's mother was wrong.

Miriam went with Aunt Abusaga and Uncle Milton to Gladys Makuma's neat mud-and-clapboard house to bring her beef tea and what comfort they could, and when they stepped into the yard there was Lucy Mawenzi, doyenne of the local healers, coming gray and shaken through the door. Inside was a wake, though Gladys Makuma wasn't dead yet. Surrounded by her children, her husband, and his stone-faced sisters, she had shrunk into herself like some artifact in the dirt. All you could see of her face was nostrils and teeth, no flesh but the flesh of a mummy, and her hands on the sheets like claws. There would be no more disco-dancing for her, no more sharing a pint of whiskey with Uncle Milton Metembe in a dark boat on the dark, pitching lake. Even an optimist could see that, and Miriam was an optimist—her mother insisted on it.

With Beryl Obote, it was even worse, because Beryl was her coeval, a girl with skinny legs and saucer eyes who wore her hair untamed and had a laugh so infectious she could bring chaos to a classroom merely by opening her mouth. Miriam was coming back from the market one afternoon, the streets a soup of mud and an army of beetles crawling over every fixed surface, when she spotted Beryl in the crowd ahead of her, the Juliana cloth like the ocean come to life and her hair a dark storm brooding over it. But something was wrong. She was lurching from side to side, taking little circumscribed steps, and people were making way for her as if she were drunk. She wasn't drunk, though when she fell to the ground, subsiding into the mud as if her legs had dissolved beneath her, Miriam saw that her eyes were as red as any drunkard's. Miriam tried to help her up—never mind the yellow tub of *matoke*, rice and beans her mother had sent her for—but Beryl couldn't find her feet, and there was a terrible smell about her. "I'm so embarrassed," she said, and if you couldn't smell it you could see it, the diarrhea and the blood seeping through the deep blue cloth into the fetid trodden mud.

After that everyone fell sick: the women who'd bought the Juliana cloth with their favors, their husbands, and their husbands' special friends, not to mention all the men who had consorted with a certain barmaid at the disco—the one who wore a *kanga* in the blue, red, and papaya of decay. It was a hex, that was what people believed at first, a spell put on them by William Wamala, who had come all the way across the lake from the homeland of their ancestral enemies—he was a sorcerer, a practitioner of the black arts, an evil spirit in the guise of a handsome and affectionate young man. But it soon became apparent that no hex, no matter how potent and far-reaching, could affect so many. No, this was a disease, one among a host of diseases in a region surfeited with them, and it seemed only natural that they call it Juliana's disease, after the cloth that had brought it to them.

Typically, it began with a headache and chills; then there was the loosening of the bowels and the progressive wasting. It could have been malaria or tuberculosis or marasmus, but it wasn't. It was something new. Something no one had ever seen before, and all who caught it—women and men in their prime, girls like Beryl Obote— were eventually wrapped up in bark cloth and sent to the grave before the breath of two months' time had been exhausted.

Uncle Milton Metembe and Aunt Abusaga contracted it at the same time, almost to the day, and Miriam moved into their house to tend them, afraid in her heart that the taint would spread to her. She cooked them soup and rice through the reek of their excrement, which flowed like stained water; she swept the house and changed their soiled sheets and read to them from the comic papers and the Bible. At night, the rats rustled in the thatch, and the things of the dark raised their voices in an unholy howl, and Miriam fell away deep into herself and listened to her aunt and uncle's tortured breathing.

The doctors came then from America, France, and England, white people in white coats, and a few who were almost white and even stranger for that, as if they'd been incompletely dipped into the milk of white life. They drew blood like vampires, vial after vial, till the sick and weary trembled at the sight of them, and still there was no cause or cure in sight, the corpses mounting, the orphans wailing; then one day the doctors went away and the government made an announcement over the radio and in the newspapers. Juliana's disease, the government said, was something new indeed, very virulent and always fatal, and it was transmitted not through cloth or hexes but through sexual contact. Distribution of condoms was being made possible by immediate implementation in every town and village, through the strenuous efforts of the government, and every man and woman, every wife and girl and special friend, should be sure of them every time sexual union was achieved. There was no other way and no other hope, short of monkhood, spinster-hood, or abstinence.

The news rocked the village. It was unthinkable. They were poor people who didn't have theaters or supermarkets or shiny big cars for diversion—they had only a plate of *dagaa*, a glass of beer, and sex, and every special friend had a special friend and there was no stop-ping it, even on pain of death. Besides which, the promised condoms never arrived, as if any true man or sensitive woman would allow a cold loop of latex rubber to come between them and pleasure in any event. People went on, almost defiantly, tempting fate, challenging it, unshakable in their conviction that though the whole world might wilt and die at their feet, they themselves would remain inviolate. The disco was as crowded as ever, the sales of beer and palm wine skyrocketed, and the corpses were shunted in a steady procession from sickbed to grave. Whatever else it might have been, it was a time of denial.

Miriam's mother was outraged. To her mind, the town's reac-tion was nothing short of suicidal. Through her position at the gov-ernment office she had been put in charge of the local campaign for safe sex, and it was her job to disseminate the unwelcome news. Though the condoms remained forever only forthcoming because of logistical problems in the capital, Miriam's mother typed a sheet of warning and reproduced it a thousand times, and a facsimile of this original soon sagged damply from every tree and post and hoarding in town. "Love Carefully," it advised, and "Zero Grazing," a somewhat confusing command borrowed from one of the innu-merable local agricultural campaigns. In fine print, it described the ravages of this very small and very dangerous thing, this virus (an entity for which there was no name in the local dialect), and what it was doing to the people of the village, the countryside, and even the capital. No one could have missed these ubiquitous sheets of warning and exhortation, and they would have had to be blind in any case to remain unaware of the plague in their midst. And deaf too. Because the chorus of lament never ceased, day or night, and you could hear it from any corner of the village and even out in the mists of the lake—a thin, steady insectile wail broken only by the desperate beat of the disco.

"Suicide," Miriam's mother snarled over breakfast one morning, while Miriam, back now from her aunt and uncle's because there was no longer any reason to be there, tried to bury her eyes in her porridge. "Irresponsible, filthy behavior. You'd think everybody in town had gone mad." The day was still fresh, standing fully revealed in the lacy limbs of the yellow-bark acacia in the front yard. Miriam's dog looked up guiltily from the mat in the corner. Somewhere a cock crowed.

A long minute ticked by, punctuated by the scrape of spoon and bowl, and then her mother rose angrily from the table and slammed her cup into the washup tub. All her fury was directed at Miriam, as if fury alone could erect a wall between an adolescent girl and James Kariango of the nicotine-stained fingers. "No better than animals in the bush," she hissed, stamping across the floorboards with hunched shoulders and ricocheting eyes, talking to the walls, to the dense, mosquito-hung air, "and no shred of self-restraint or respect even."

Miriam wasn't listening. Her mother's rhetoric was as empty as a bucket in a dry well. What did *she* know? Sex to her mother was a memory. "That itch," she called it, as if it were something you caught from a poisonous leaf or a clump of nettles, but she never itched and as far as Miriam could see she'd as soon have a hyena in the house as a special friend. Miriam understood what her mother was telling her, she heard the fear seeping through the fierceness of that repetitive and concussive voice, and she knew how immortally lucky she was that William Wamala hadn't found her pretty enough to bother with. She understood all that and she was scared, the pleading eyes of Beryl Obote, Aunt Abusaga, Uncle Milton Metembe, and all the rest unsettling her dreams and quickening her pace through the market, but when James Kariango crept around back of the house fifteen minutes later and raised two yellowed fingers to his lips and whistled like an innocuous little bird, she was out the door before the sweat had time to sprout under her arms.

The first time he'd come around, indestructible with his new shoulders, jaunty and confident and fingering a thin silver chain at his throat, Miriam's mother had chased him down the front steps at the point of a paring knife, cursing into the trees till every head in the neighborhood was turned and every ear attuned. Tending Aunt Abusaga and Uncle Milton Metembe had in its way been Miriam's penance for attracting such a boy—any boy—and she'd been safe there among the walking dead and the weight of their sorrows. But now she was home and the months had gone by and James Kariango, that perfect specimen, was irresistible.

Her mother had gone off to work. Her dog was asleep. The eyes of the world were turned to the market and the laundry and a hundred other things. It was very, very early, and the taste of James Kariango's lips was like the taste of the sweetest fruit, mango and papaya and the sweet dripping syrup of fresh-cut pineapple. She kissed him there, behind the house, where the flowers grew thick and the lizards scuttered through the dirt and held their tails high in sign of some fleeting triumph. And then, after a long while, every pore of her body opening up like a desert plant at the first hint of rain, she led him inside.

He was very solemn. Very gentle. Every touch was electric, his fingers plugged into some internal socket, his face glowing like the ball at the disco. She let him strip off her clothes and she watched in fear and anticipation as he stepped out of his shorts and revealed himself to her. The fear was real. It was palpable. It meant the whole world and all of life. But then he laid her down in the familiar cradle of her bed and hovered over her in all of his glory, and, oh, it felt so good.

(1997)

HEART OF A CHAMPION

We scan the cornfields and the wheatfields winking gold and gold-brown and yellowbrown in the midday sun, on up the grassy slope to the barn redder than red against the sky bluer than blue, across the smooth stretch of the barnyard with its pecking chickens, and then right on up to the screen door at the back of the house. The door swings open, a black hole in the sun, and Timmy emerges with his corn-silk hair, corn-fed face. He is dressed in crisp overalls, striped T-shirt, stubby blue Keds. There'd have to be a breeze—and we're not disappointed—his clean fine cup-cut hair waves and settles as he scuffs across the barnyard and out to the edge of the field. The boy stops there to gaze out over the nodding wheat, eyes unsquinted despite the sun, and blue as tinted lenses. Then he brings three fingers to his lips in a neat triangle and whistles long and low, sloping up sharp to cut off at the peak. A moment passes: he whistles again. And then we see it—way out there at the far corner of the field—the ripple, the dashing furrow, the blur of the streaking dog, white chest, flashing feet.

They're in the woods now. The boy whistling, hands in pockets, kicking along with his short baby-fat strides; the dog beside him wagging the white tip of her tail like an all-clear flag. They pass beneath an arching old black-barked oak. It creaks. And suddenly begins to fling itself down on them: immense, brutal: a panzer strike.

The boy's eyes startle and then there's a blur, a smart snout clutching his pant leg, the thunderblast of the trunk, the dust and spinning leaves. "Golly, Lassie . . . I didn't even see it," says the boy sitting safe in a mound of moss. The collie looks up at him (the svelte snout, the deep gold logician's eyes), and laps at his face.

And now they're down by the river. The water is brown with angry suppurations, spiked with branches, fence posts, tires, and logs. It rushes like the sides of boxcars—and chews deep and insidious at the bank under Timmy's feet. The roar is like a jetport: little wonder he can't hear the dog's warning bark. We watch the crack appear, widen to a ditch; then the halves separating (snatch of red earth, writhe of worm), the poise and pitch, and Timmy crashing down with it. Just a flash—but already he's way downstream, his head like a plastic jug, dashed and bobbed, spinning toward the nasty mouth of the falls. But there's the dog—fast as a struck match—bursting along the bank all white and gold melded in motion, hair sleeked with the wind of it, legs beating time to the panting score. . . . Yet what can she hope to do?—the current surges on, lengths ahead, sure bet to win the race to the falls. Timmy sweeps closer, sweeps closer, the falls loud now as a hundred timpani, the war drums of the Sioux, Africa gone bloodlust mad! The dog strains, lashing over the wet earth like a whipcrack; strains every last ganglion and dendrite until finally she draws abreast of him. Then she's in the air, the foaming yellow water. Her paws churning like pistons, whiskers chuffing with the exertion—oh the roar!—and there, she's got him, her sure jaws clamping down on the shirt collar, her eyes fixed on the slip of rock at the falls' edge. Our blood races, organs palpitate. The black brink of the falls, the white paws digging at the rock—and then they're safe. The collie sniffs at Timmy's inert little form, nudges his side until she manages to roll him over. Then clears his tongue and begins mouth-to-mouth.

Night: the barnyard still, a bulb burning over the screen door. Inside, the family sit at dinner, the table heaped with pork chops, mashed potatoes, applesauce and peas, a pitcher of clean white milk. Home-baked bread. Mom and Dad, their faces sexless, bland, perpetually good-humored and sympathetic, poise stiff-backed, forks in mid-swoop, while Timmy tells his story: "So then Lassie grabbed me by the collar and golly I musta blanked out cause I don't remember anything more till I woke up on the rock—"

"Well I'll be," says Mom.

"You're lucky you've got such a good dog, son," says Dad, gazing down at the collie where she lies patiently, snout over paw, tail wapping the floor. She is combed and washed and fluffed, her lashes mascaraed and curled, her chest and paws white as dishsoap. She looks up humbly. But then her ears leap, her neck jerks round—and she's up at the door, head cocked, alert. A high yipping yowl like a stuttering fire whistle shudders through the room. And then another. The dog whines.

"Darn," says Dad. "I thought we were rid of those coyotes—next thing they'll be after the chickens again."

The moon blanches the yard, leans black shadows on the trees, the barn. Upstairs in the house, Timmy lies sleeping in the pale light, his hair fastidiously mussed, his breathing gentle. The collie lies on the throw rug beside the bed. We see that her eyes are open. Suddenly she rises and slips to the window, silent as a shadow. And looks down the long elegant snout to the barnyard below, where the coyote slinks from shade to shade, a limp pullet dangling from his jaws. He is stunted, scabious, syphilitic, his forepaw trap-twisted, his eyes running. The collie whimpers softly from behind the window. And the coyote stops in mid-trot, frozen in a cold shard of light, ears high on his head. Then drops the chicken at his feet, leers up at the window and begins a soft, crooning, sad-faced song.

The screen door slaps behind Timmy as he bolts from the house, Lassie at his heels. Mom's head emerges on the rebound. "Timmy!"

(He stops as if jerked by a rope, turns to face her.) "You be home before lunch, hear?"

"Sure, Mom," he says, already spinning off, the dog by his side. We get a close-up of Mom's face: she is smiling a benevolent boys-will-be-boys smile. Her teeth are perfect.

In the woods Timmy steps on a rattler and the dog bites its head off. "Gosh," he says. "Good girl, Lassie." Then he stumbles and slips over an embankment, rolls down the brushy incline and over a sudden precipice, whirling out into the breathtaking blue space like a skydiver. He thumps down on a narrow ledge twenty feet below. And immediately scrambles to his feet, peering timorously down the sheer wall to the heap of bleached bone at its base. Small stones break loose, shoot out like asteroids. Dirt-slides begin. But Lassie yarps reassuringly from above, sprints back to the barn for a winch and cable, hoists the boy to safety.

On their way back for lunch Timmy leads them through a still and leaf-darkened copse. We remark how odd it is that the birds and crickets have left off their cheeping, how puzzling that the background music has begun to rumble so. Suddenly, round a bend in the path before them, the coyote appears. Nose to the ground, intent, unaware of them. But all at once he jerks to a halt, shudders like an epileptic, the hackles rising, tail dipping between his legs. The collie too stops short, just yards away, her chest proud and shaggy and white. The coyote cowers, bunches like a cat, glares at them. Timmy's face sags with alarm. The coyote lifts his lip. But then, instead of leaping at her adversary's throat, the collie prances up and stretches her nose out to him, her eyes soft as a leading lady's, round as a doe's. She's balsamed and perfumed; her full chest tapers a lovely S to her sleek haunches and sculpted legs. He is puny, runted, half her size, his coat like a discarded doormat. She circles him now, sniffing. She whimpers, he growls: throaty and tough, the bad guy. And stands stiff while she licks at his whiskers, noses at his rear, the bald black scrotum. Timmy is horror-struck. Then, the music sweeping off in birdtrills of flute and harpstring, the coyote slips round behind, throat thrown back, black lips tight with anticipation.

"What was she doing, Dad?" Timmy asks over his milk and sandwich.

"The sky was blue today, son," he says.

"But she had him trapped, Dad—they were stuck together end to end and I thought we had that wicked old coyote but then she went and let him go—what's got into her, Dad?"

"The barn was red today, son," he says.

Late afternoon: the sun mellow, more orange than white. Purpling clots of shadow hang from the branches, ravel out from the tree trunks. Bees and wasps and flies saw away at the wet full-bellied air. Timmy and the dog are far out beyond the north pasture, out by the old Indian burial mound, where the boy stoops now to search for arrowheads. Oddly, the collie is not watching him: instead she's pacing the crest above, whimpering softly, pausing from time to time to stare out across the forest, her eyes distant and moonstruck. Behind her, storm clouds squat on the horizon like dark kidneys or brains.

We observe the wind kicking up: leaves flapping like wash, saplings quivering, weeds whipping. It darkens quickly now, the clouds scudding low and smoky over the treetops, blotting the sun from view. Lassie's white is whiter than ever, highlighted against the dark horizon, the wind-whipped hair foaming around her. Still she doesn't look down at the boy: he digs, dirty-kneed, stoop-backed, oblivious. Then the first fat random drops, a flash, the volcanic blast of thunder. Timmy glances over his shoulder at the noise: he's just in time to watch the scorched pine plummeting toward the constellated freckles in the center of his forehead. Now the collie turns—too late!—the *swoosh-whack!* of the tree, the trembling needles. She's there in an instant, tearing at the green welter, struggling through to his side. He lies unconscious in the muddying earth, hair artistically

arranged, a thin scratch painted on his cheek. The trunk lies across the small of his back like the tail of a brontosaurus. The rain falls.

Lassie tugs doggedly at a knob in the trunk, her pretty paws slipping in the wet—but it's no use—it would take a block and tackle, a crane, an army of Bunyans to shift that stubborn bulk. She falters, licks at his ear, whimpers. We observe the troubled look in her eye as she hesitates, uncertain, priorities warring: should she stand guard, or dash for help? The decision is sure and swift—her eyes firm with purpose and she is off like a shard of shrapnel, already up the hill, shooting past the dripping trees, over the river, already cleaving through the high wet banks of wheat.

A moment later she's dashing through the puddled and rain-screened barnyard, barking right on up to the back door, where she pauses to scratch daintily, her voice high-pitched and insistent. Mom swings open the door and the collie pads in, claws clacking on the shiny linoleum. "What is it, girl? What's the matter? Where's Timmy?"

"Yarf! Yarfata-yarf-yarf!"

"Oh my! Dad! Dad, come quickly!"

Dad rushes in, his face stolid and reassuring as the Lincoln Memorial. "What is it, dear? . . . Why, Lassie?"

"Oh Dad, Timmy's trapped under a pine tree out by the old Indian burial ground—"

"Arpit-arp."

"—a mile and a half past the north pasture."

Dad is quick, firm, decisive. "Lassie—you get back up there and stand watch over Timmy. . . . Mom and I'll go for Doc Walker. Hurry now!"

The collie hesitates at the door: "Rarf-arrar-ra!"

"Right," says Dad. "Mom, fetch the chain saw."

We're back in the woods now. A shot of the mud-running burial mound locates us—yes, there's the fallen pine, and there: Timmy. He

lies in a puddle, eyes closed, breathing slow. The hiss of the rain is loud as static. We see it at work: scattering leaves, digging trenches, inciting streams to swallow their banks. It lies deep now in the low areas, and in the mid areas, and in the high areas. Then a shot of the dam, some indeterminate (but short we presume) distance off, the yellow water churning over its lip like urine, the ugly earthen belly distended, blistered with the pressure. Raindrops pock the surface like a plague.

Suddenly the music plunges to those thunderous crouching chords—we're back at the pine now—what is it? There: the coyote. Sniffing, furtive, the malicious eyes, the crouch and slink. He stiffens when he spots the boy—but then slouches closer, a rubbery dangle drooling from between his mismeshed teeth. Closer. Right over the prone figure now, those ominous chords setting up ominous vibrations in our bowels. He stoops, head dipping between his shoulders, irises caught in the corners of his eyes: wary, sly, predatory: the vulture slavering over the fallen fawn.

But wait!—here comes the collie, sprinting out of the wheatfield, bounding rock to rock across the crazed river, her limbs contourless with sheer speed and purpose, the music racing in a mad heroic prestissimo!

The jolting front seat of a Ford. Dad, Mom, and the Doctor, all dressed in rain slickers and flap-brimmed rain hats, sitting shoulder to shoulder behind the clapping wipers. Their jaws set with determination, eyes aflicker with pioneer gumption.

The coyote's jaws, serrated grinders, work at the tough bone and cartilage of Timmy's left hand. The boy's eyelids flutter with the pain, and he lifts his head feebly—but almost immediately it slaps down again, flat and volitionless, in the mud. At that instant Lassie blazes over the hill like a cavalry charge, show-dog indignation aflame in her eyes. The scrag of a coyote looks up at her, drooling

blood, choking down frantic bits of flesh. Looks up at her from eyes that go back thirty million years, savage and bloodlustful and free. Looks up unmoved, uncringing, the bloody snout and steady yellow eyes less a physical challenge than philosophical. We watch the collie's expression alter in mid-bound—the look of offended AKC morality giving way, dissolving. She skids to a halt, drops her tail and approaches him, a buttery gaze in her golden eyes. She licks the blood from his lips.

The dam. Impossibly swollen, rain festering the yellow surface, a hundred new streams a minute rampaging in, the pressure of those millions of gallons hard-punching those millions more. There! the first gap, the water spewing out, a burst bubo. And now the dam shudders, splinters, falls to pieces like so much cheap pottery. The roar is devastating.

The two animals start at that terrible rumbling, and, still working their gummy jaws, they dash up the far side of the hill. We watch the white-tipped tail retreating side by side with the hacked and tick-blistered gray one—wagging like raggled banners as they disappear into the trees at the top of the rise. We're left with a tableau: the rain, the fallen pine in the crotch of the valley's V, the spot of the boy's head. And that chilling roar in our ears. Suddenly the wall of water appears at the far end of the V, smashing through the little declivity like a god-sized fist, prickling with shattered trunks and boulders, grinding along like a quick-melted glacier, like planets in collision. We cut to Timmy: eyes closed, hair plastered, his left arm looking as though it should be wrapped in butcher's paper. How? we wonder. How will they ever get him out of this? But then we see them—Mom, Dad, and the Doctor—struggling up that same rise, rushing with the frenetic music now, the torrent seething closer, booming and howling. Dad launches himself in full charge down the hillside—but the water is already sweeping over the fallen pine, lifting it like paper—there's a blur, a quick clip of a typhoon at sea (is that a flash of blond hair?), and it's over. The valley is filled to the top of the rise, the water ribbed and rushing like the Colorado in adolescence. Dad's pants are wet to the crotch.

Mom's face, the Doctor's. Rain. And then the opening strains of the theme song, one violin at first, swelling in mournful mid-American triumph as the full orchestra comes in, tearful, beautiful, heroic, sweeping us up and out of the dismal rain, back to the golden wheatfields in the midday sun. The boy cups his hands to his mouth and pipes: "Laahh-sie! Laahh-sie!" And then we see it—way out there at the end of the field—the ripple, the dashing furrow, the blur of the streaking dog, white chest, flashing feet.

(1974)

AFTERWORD

Fun. How often have you heard that term used to describe the books and stories assigned in literature classes today? Not so often, I would think. Because what so many of our beard-tugging critics and the long-suffering students in our secondary schools and colleges seem to have lost sight of is that stories are meant as entertainment. Not as literary documents to be dissected by professors, and certainly not as homework or the basis of the dreaded essay assignment. Stories—literature—should be a joy, fun, as much a secret means of access to the true and scintillating world as the latest CD or head-spinning Hollywood movie. My stories have always grown out of my own pure joy in the power of storytelling, and the selection here should, I hope, appeal to the subversive wit and percolating intelligence of teenagers everywhere, especially those who don't mind shutting the rest of the world out and entering my slippery, surreal universe for a strange and precious hour or two.

The first of the pieces here, "The Human Fly," came to me, as many stories do, in a jumble of impressions. I had heard of a daredevil similar to "La Mosca Humana," a man who, for some unfathomable reason, felt that he had to scale skyscrapers with not much more than his fingernails, teeth, and clenched toes to support him. And I knew a Hollywood talent agent who did deal with the odd and talentless acts no one else would touch. And finally, as I began to write the first sentence—"In the early days, before the press took him up, his outfit was pretty basic: tights and cape, plastic swim goggles and a bathing cap in the brightest shade of red he could find"—I realized that this was a story about a man who wanted, above all else, fame. I myself had been criticized in the press for my cavalier attitude toward the forms and proprieties of the literary interview, and for my hunger for fame. So: I am like Zoltan, but instead of the moth-eaten tights of the comic book superhero, I wear a black leather jacket and a goatee.

But, unlike me, Zoltan wants to be famous simply for the idea of fame itself. He doesn't produce anything—no music, no art, no writing or videos. I suppose he's a kind of performance artist, as all daredevils are, but in his quest for fame he is risking his skinny bones and battered flesh. And, of course, in such a story, escalation plays a big part—each new feat must top the last. The fans are fickle, after all, and the artist, like Kafka's Hunger Artist, feels a need not only to appeal to them afresh, but to exceed himself and anyone else who has ever attempted the same feats. For Zoltan, almost inevitably, the struggle will end badly. Why? Is it because superheroes only exist in comic books? Or is it that Zoltan, despite his reincarnation in an animated cartoon, isn't really a hero at all? Has he got his wires crossed? Is he crazy? Are all artists crazy? I leave that for you to decide.

I don't often write autobiographical stories—I'd rather dream on the page than mine my own pedestrian life for material—but sometimes strong autobiographical elements do form the foundation for a story. "The Fog Man" is a case in point. I grew up in a suburban neighborhood very much like the one described here, I had a close friend who, like Casper, always pushed the limits in the most perverse and seductive ways, and the scene regarding the dance and the mother—my mother—is true to life. The rest, though, is the invented fabric that takes unformed experience and makes a story out of it that can speak to anyone.

Next up is "Rara Avis," a story set in that same remembered past. The dredged-up incident that provides the reason for the story is an incident so vague and so deeply buried in my childhood it has become a sort of dream. Yes, a rare bird landed on the roof of the furniture store and yes the whole neighborhood turned out to marvel at it. But what did it mean and why do I remember it, even if imperfectly? I discovered the answer in the bird's secret wound—a Freudian wound—and realized that on the dream level this is a coming-of-age story. I suppose we're not all equally ready to come of age, to join the adult world, with its mysteries of sexual intrigue, and that last hard line seems to underscore it, at least for the narrator. Perhaps not consciously, but in a deeper way, a lyrical, psychosexual, almost mythic way.

The fourth story, "The Champ," is one of my earliest. I wrote this, along with "Heart of a Champion" and the other stories from my first book, while I was in college, as a grad student at the University of Iowa Writers' Workshop. As you can see, the format is that of a boxing match, but instead we have an eating contest, replete with the dissing and taunts we now see athletes tossing around as a matter of course. Kid Gullet's poetic taunt of Angelo D., incidentally, is both a parody of and homage to the great boxer, Mohammed Ali, who routinely put down his opponents in like fashion. The fun of the story is in the absurdity of the concept, of course, but it does talk to a culture in which such superabundance makes an eating contest possible in the first place (and for the protestors' chant of "Remember Biafra," we can substitute Somalia, Rwanda, or Indonesia, because sadly, the same privation still prevails).

The fifth story, "Beat," is a satiric (and yet, I hope, affectionate) look at Jack Kerouac and the foundations of the Beat Movement. I did my homework here to the extent of knowing where Kerouac was living at Christmas in 1957 (and in what sad condition too) and where the other major Beat figures you meet here were as well.

Thus, we have Allen Ginsburg, William Burroughs, and (yes, he was in jail at the time) Neal Cassady. I like to read this one aloud to an audience. It has a real beat to it, almost like a rap, and that beat and the ravishing, over-the-top language is part of the real, true, and veritable fun the author is having here.

Next in line is "Greasy Lake," my best-known and most frequently anthologized story. This is the one that practically all highschool and college students find in their literature texts, and then need to confront for purposes of the exegetic essay. Sorry, folks—I don't mean to inflict such academic rigors on you. The story is meant to be read and enjoyed on its own terms, but, of course, like all good stories, "Greasy Lake" provokes you to think about the consequences of the characters' actions—in this case, the quest for cool and the undying appeal of hip. I wrote the story in the early eighties, and it was inspired by the free and jubilant teen anthems of Bruce Springsteen, who provides the epigraph for the story. I've purposely kept the time period of the story a bit vague (any teen could have a classic Chevy or listen to reggae), so that it can be universally received. That is, everyone has been down to Greasy Lake, wherever that greasy lake may be, and everyone has wanted that something indefinable in the night, the richness of experience, of sex, drugs, alcohol, nature, the hard beating of the unformed heart, and the screaming, megawatt power of hip.

The next story, "The Love of My Life," which appeared in *The New Yorker* a few years ago, provoked more reaction than perhaps any piece I've ever done. It was inspired by an actual incident that was widely covered in the news and I've stuck close to the facts as reported, but what the facts don't give us is the why. I wanted to find out what it might be like to be those doomed lovers and to understand what it would take to toss that newborn baby into the Dumpster and how life can be so terrible and beautiful at the same time. (Incidentally, when the story was first published, two freshman came into my office at USC just to meet me and say that they were moved by the power of the story. I was very pleased, of course, and I thanked them. There was a moment of silence, then one of them asked, "How do you know so much about teenagers?" And I, with a sly and knowing grin, leaned across the desk and revealed that many eons ago, when woolly mammoths still lumbered across the earth and the skies were on fire, I too was a teenager.)

The eighth story here, "Achates McNeil," is one of the two stories I've ever written that came to me in some form as early-morning dreams (the other is "Bloodfall," from my first book, *Descent of Man*). I was up in the mountains during the holiday season, looking out on great fat-bottomed sequoias stuck up to their ankles in snow and snuffing that turkey a-roasting in the pan, and I thought of my own three children, who were then very young—preteens. I wondered what it might be like for them to grow into adolescence and beyond in the (potential) shadow of a famous parent. And so I devised a fiction to address it, and if a writer who physically resembles me appears here in all his caricatured glory, please don't mistake him for the author of this book or his family situation—and insufferable ego—for mine. No, no, no, I'm not that sort of writer at all. Or, well, just a tiny little bit?

"56-0" is pure fun. You'll find a satiric thrust here too, of course, but as the story evolved I saw that it was going to address the conventional wisdom about our participation in sports. (I do love sports, by the way, and played sports in high school and college.) One morning, glancing through the paper, I saw that one college football team had lost by the score that became the title of this story, and I began to wonder just what such a drubbing teaches you. Does it inculcate valuable lessons? Teach you to be a good sport? Deepen your character? Or does it teach you that life is defeat, that no matter what you do or how hard you try, you will always lose and that losing is the lot of every man, woman, and child on this earth? Just wondering, that's all.

Speaking of satire, "The Hit Man" has proven popular over the years because of its parody of such types—the mafioso hidden behind the screen or wearing a black hood in order to protect his identity—as they are delivered up to us in films and on TV. It's a simple step, if your mind works that way, to add the absurd element of the permanent hood and to think in terms of passing the family profession down through the generations. Whatever you think of the story, certainly you'll have to admit that the teenaged Hit Man sure knows how to take a girl out on a date.

"Almost Shooting an Elephant" is a new story, just written this year. I often find that stories are inspired by two or more elements and that sometimes those elements in conjunction strengthen and deepen the focus of the piece or give it another dimension. This was the case here. Again, I was reading the newspaper—a time-honored tradition and one that brings a whole parade of horror and absurdity across the breakfast table each morning—and discovered a little paragraph about some elephants in India who'd come storming out of the jungle in order to get at the villagers' stock of beer. What a concept! Drunken elephants! I leapt up from the table with a shout. But what's the context? I wondered. It took me a while, but then I thought of George Orwell's astonishingly rigorous and powerful piece of reportage, "Shooting an Elephant," and I had my inspiration. The result may be enjoyable in large part because it is a fish-out-of-water story, featuring a fairly clueless narrator, the aforementioned drunken elephants, and one very appealing girl with a consummately lovely navel. Oh, yes, and how could I forget: the *bhut* himself?

The penultimate story, "Juliana Cloth," was inspired in part by accounts of the emergence of new pathogens and the war for dominance being fought daily in our bodies. I had read accounts of the initial spread of AIDS in Africa and once again, wanting to know the why and how of its transmission, I wrote a story in order to find out. In this telling, our heroine, no matter what advice she's been given or how often her elders have warned and berated her, cannot resist the pull of her own desire, as who can? We can be told of the dangers of various behaviors, we can be scared and scandalized and brain-washed, but is there any substitute for the power of experience? No, not even when it proves fatal (as in this story it may or may not).

Speaking of power, what about the power of the little screen that hovers over every living room in the industrialized world like some sort of electronic totem? TV, yes, I'm speaking of TV. I am the first of the TV generation, and until I was seventeen and away at college, I didn't find my stories in books, but on the little screen, where they were fed to me pixel by pixel, like the inane commercials that made them possible. But what did that mean, and why, once I'd discovered another kind of life, did I go cold turkey on that insidious medium? Well, in order to find out, I wrote a little satire called "Heart of a Champion." I had seen the foursquare families presented in show after show, the happy smiles and the rich if bland enjoyment of the American lifestyle, and it didn't conform to anything I knew. That made me depressed. It made me angry. And further, with a show like *Lassie*, it made me wonder just what this ideal bond between species—boy *Homo sapiens* and female *Canis familiaris*—really meant. Why would a dog suppress its instincts in order to serve its human masters? How smart is a dog, anyhow (look at the sequence where Lassie barks out her very precise message)? You will also notice that the story takes the form of an episode of this show, and its satire is meant to expose some of the comforting and banal myths TV promulgates. Timmy dies in my version, an event that would be utterly unthinkable to the creators of such shows, and yet he is blithely resurrected at the end in time for the theme song to ring out over the airwaves: there is no savagery and there is no death in TV-land. Yes, but have you ever stopped to wonder about the dogs, the geckos, the coyotes and lions and seals: what are they thinking?

—T. C. Boyle
Santa Barbara, California

Grateful acknowledgment is made to the following magazines, in which these stories first appeared:

"Achates McNeil," "Juliana Cloth," and "The Love of My Life," *The New Yorker*
"Almost Shooting an Elephant," *Zoetrope: All-Story*
"Rara Avis," *Antaeus*
"Heart of a Champion," *Esquire*
"The Champ," *The Atlantic Monthly*
"56-0," "Beat," and "The Human Fly," *Playboy*
"The Fog Man," *Gentleman's Quarterly*
"The Hit Man," *North American Review*
"Greasy Lake," *The Paris Review*

"The Love of My Life" also appeared in *Prize Stories 2001: The O. Henry Awards*, edited by Larry Dark (Anchor Books); "The Love of My Life" and "Achates McNeil," in *After the Plague* (Penguin); "Rara Avis" and "Greasy Lake," in *Greasy Lake and Other Stories* and *T. C. Boyle Stories* (both Penguin); "Heart of a Champion" and "The Champ," in *Descent of Man* and *T. C. Boyle Stories* (both Penguin); "The Human Fly," in *If the River Was Whiskey* and *T. C. Boyle Stories* (both Penguin); "The Fog Man," "Beat," and "56-0," in *Without a Hero* and *T. C. Boyle Stories* (both Penguin); and "The Hit Man" and "Juliana Cloth," in *T. C. Boyle Stories* (Penguin).

Grateful acknowledgment is made to the following for permission to reprint copyrighted material: *Bruce Springsteen/ Jon Landau Management, Inc.*: Lyrics from "Spirit in the Night," by Bruce Springsteen. Copyright © 1972 by Bruce Springsteen. All rights reserved.